"You don't know me," I said

"Aye, and we don't want to," the tall boy declared. "It's your sort come and turn the milk, make the dogs howl all night, and cause the mare to miscarry, so my dad says."

I'd never met this boy's dad and already I disliked him.

By now, I was balanced on my feet and weighing my chances of breaking free. The tall boy might be bigger than me, but life with Sir had made me tough. If I could break through their circle, I thought I could outrun them.

A big if.

"How do you know it's a faerie, George?"

"Look at it. Too tall for a pixie, too pale for a brownie, and those ears, like Agnes says. Those ears are a dead giveaway."

The other girl whispered, "Might be an elf."

Something in her voice swiveled my head so I could look at her—she stood nearly behind me. Her voice sounded beautiful, like the wind over the moor when it's feeling playful, or like one of the songs I sang to myself.

And I saw she was beautiful, with light brown hair streaked blonde by the summer sun, and gentle eyes.

But George denied it. "Nay—elves are pleasant-looking. Does that look pleasant to you, Mallie?"

Mallie. I tucked her name away in my heart.

Rum Paul Stillskin

by

Laura Strickland

Rum Paul Stillskin

Cover Art by *Diana Carlile*

The Wild Rose Press, Inc.
PO Box 708
Adams Basin, NY 14410-0708
Visit us at www.thewildrosepress.com

Publishing History
First Fantasy Rose Edition, 2019
Print ISBN 978-1-5092-2612-2
Digital ISBN 978-1-5092-2613-9

Published in the United States of America

Dedication

For all those who doubt they deserve love.

Books by Laura Strickland
published by The Wild Rose Press, Inc.

Hearts of Caledonia Series:
Loyal and True, Book One
Valiant and Wise, Book Two
Noble and Blessed, Book Three
The Guardians of Sherwood Trilogy:
Daughter of Sherwood, Book One
Champion of Sherwood, Book Two
Lord of Sherwood, Book Three
Dead Handsome: A Buffalo Steampunk Adventure
Off Kilter: A Buffalo Steampunk Adventure
Sheer Madness: A Buffalo Steampunk Adventure
Steel Kisses: A Buffalo Steampunk Adventure
Tough Prospect: A Buffalo Steampunk Adventure
Devil Black
His Wicked Highland Ways
One Enchanted Scottish Knight
Honor Bound: A Highland Adventure
The Hiring Fair
The White Gull
Forged by Love (sequel to *The White Gull*)
Words and Dreams (sequel to *Forged by Love*)
Stars in the Morning
Awake on Garland Street
Cinder-Ugly
Rum Paul Stillskin
Mrs. Claus and the Viking Ship
The Tenth Suitor
Christmastime on Donner's Mountain
Ask Me (part of the Candy Hearts Series)

Part One

Laura Strickland

Chapter One

What's in a name? Over the course of my life, I've had any number of appellations thrown at me. I must have heard every manner of insult and slur. And, my life being what it is, with me fated to live so much of it over and over again, the years have been many, and long.

I am here to tell you now, when all is said and done, a name is but a name—a label—and means little. It is the heart of a man, or woman for all that, which matters. Some hearts are true and some empty of truth, and you cannot always tell the difference just by looking.

Born around the year 1620 and then abandoned under the proverbial cabbage leaf, I no longer remember the exact day of my birth. An old woman found me lying half hidden in her garden when she went out to hoe her vegetables and, being kind of nature, took me back to her husband, a drunkard.

This happened back in the days when folk still believed in the Fae, when the church had but a tentative hold on the land, and spirits walked the downs. These two old folks lived isolated, away from the town, yet believed they shared that bleak moor with others, unseen. So when the old woman brought me in out of the misty morning and showed me to her husband, who'd been busy drinking all night long, he stared at me blearily and at once declared, "Woman, that's an elf child."

"Do you think so?" she asked uncertainly, peering down at me lying wrapped in her shawl. "It's a wee boy, and he looks new born."

"Throw it outside," advised the man callously.

"'Twill surely die if I do."

"It will bring all manner of trouble, if you don't."

Perhaps she should have listened to him. Had I perished then, in the damp beneath the cabbage plant, it might have prevented all the heartache that followed. But the old woman had never had a child of her own, so she sat with me on her knee while outside it began to rain and blow, and she told herself she couldn't be so heartless as to put me out.

When the old man roused from his drunken doze much later and saw me still there beneath his roof, he cried, "Aye, that's a rum thing."

So they called me Rum. I called them *Ma* and *Sir* when I grew old enough to speak. According to Ma, it did not take me long; I began jabbering before I could crawl, and learned words at an unnatural rate.

"Always clever with words and games and riddles," she told me later.

It was as well I'd been blessed with a good brain, for I had not much else about which I might brag. As I grew, it became all too painfully evident I was not human, or at least not entirely human. My head was long and narrow, and my ears came to exaggerated points. My arms and legs grew narrow also and looked fragile, though I possessed prodigious strength and could accomplish vast amounts of work if I chose, which I rarely did.

The old woman treated me kindly, even though she often speculated aloud as to what I might be. The old man was the first to give me a string of ugly names—everything he could imagine, from "a bad-un" to "lazy, no-good elf."

"He cannot be an elf, after all," Ma would protest earnestly, and thoughtlessly. "Elves are beautiful."

She did not pause to think about injuring my feelings. Neither of them did. In their eyes, I had no right to the sort of conceit that might take offense. The lowest of the low I was and, as Sir frequently declared, lucky he gave me house room.

The room he did give me was part of the loft, up under the thatched roof. The rest of the loft served as storage for everything from old clothes to broken furniture. Among these I eventually discovered a chest that contained relics from Sir's youth when he'd gone to sea. But that had been long ago. When I knew him, he only occasionally stumped away across the downs upon some undisclosed business, and spent most of his time drunk there beside the fire, swearing and quite often throwing things at me.

Ma did all the actual work around the place, caring for our lone cow and the hogs, when we had them. She kept chickens and sometimes traded the eggs for things she couldn't afford to buy. She scrubbed and spun wool and worked most of the hours that came her way.

I should have helped more than I did, given she showed me the only affection I ever saw. When I got old enough, she taught me how to do most of the chores, including the spinning.

Truth was, I hated being confined to any sort of work. I possessed great amounts of energy and could, as I say, accomplish much if I chose. But spinning, chopping wood, and splitting kindling bored me. Planting or hoeing the garden made me feel itchy and wild.

I liked to while away my time out on the downs, or sitting by the fire, on the rare occasions Sir wasn't there ahead of me. I loved staring into the flames and watching the pictures that formed, moved, and changed.

If Sir caught me at it, he would clout me on the head and swear at me. "That's a rum occupation for a young lad, Rum," he'd sneer. "What do you think you are, a goblin?"

I didn't know what I was, but I spent considerable time thinking on it. In many ways, I seemed human. I had five fingers on each hand and five toes on each foot. But I could tell I wasn't like anyone else. Sometimes Ma took me to the village with her, and I saw other children there. The ones who were near my size, and so presumably near my age, seemed put together differently. Their legs were shorter, their bodies sturdier. Their hair lay flat on their heads or fell to their shoulders in fetching curls.

My hair did not. It stuck up all over my head—Ma had never found a comb or brush that could make it lie down—and was black as the coal clunkers at the bottom of the fire.

None of the other children had sharp, clever faces like mine either, or eyes that tipped up at the outer corners, as green as new fern leaves ready to unfurl. None of them could talk as quickly or run as fast as I could. And none of them showed any inclination to play with me. Instead they stood about with their thumbs in their mouths, fixing me with empty stares.

"What is he?" I heard women ask Ma more than once.

She inevitably answered, "Why, a boy, of course."

They would shake their heads and lower their voices. "That ain't no boy."

Didn't they know that lowering their voices did no good? I could hear a vole stir in the grass at fifty paces, could hear what the wind said when it swept across the downs. I could hear what Ma and Sir said about me, all the way up in the loft.

They said—

We can't keep him. He grows unnatural, like.

I cannot throw him out into the world.

You never should have brought him in, in the first place. I told you so that first morning.

'Tis a sin to let a creature die.

Not a creature such as that. Mark me, woman, he will slit our throats in our beds some night.

I lay and thought about it, the prospect of slitting their throats. I knew where Ma kept the knives. And Sir had a flick blade he wore in his boot, and left there when he took the boots off. For that matter, I could use the axe.

He's a good boy.

He is not. He is turning into something neither you nor I want to see.

Maybe we should send him to chapel.

Aye, if you want the roof to fall in on him.

He needs to go to school.

I doubt they'll have him, Martha.

Martha was Ma's real name.

Besides, he's already too clever for his own good— and ours.

Husband…what do you think he is?

Ma never got an answer to that question. At least, I usually fell asleep before I heard one.

I would dream deep dreams then, of fire, the light of a great beacon reaching high into the sky. The fire contained pictures just like the ones that danced in the hearth, only harder to see. I thought that perhaps people lived in the fire and had answers to all my questions.

Perhaps they were like me, those folk.

But one of the first things Ma had taught me was: Don't touch the fire. It hurts. It burns.

'Twould be entirely mad, then, to leap clear into the flames, searching for others like myself.

Chapter Two

Names, so they say, are magical. I never had any trouble believing in magic. In fact, it seemed inconceivable to me that anyone could fail to believe in it.

How could a person disbelieve a power that made grass sprout and grow green? That caused a radish to spring up from a tiny seed and become red? That taught the birds to sing and brought the rain when the earth needed it?

Of course magic existed.

Even Ma and Sir believed in it. Ma often left a tiny dish of milk out for the faeries, though I knew for a fact the cat drank it. Sir frequently made the sign against evil, often when I walked into the room unexpectedly.

To be sure, Sir also made that sign at the pastor of the village chapel when he came calling. Reverend Rogers did not darken the door of Sir's humble cottage often. By the time I was eight or so, I'd seen the fellow there perhaps two or three times that I could recall.

But it does stand out quite vividly in my mind how he came toddling up the path to the door one sunny afternoon, perhaps because his visit served to define so much for me.

A small man with muttonchop whiskers and tiny eyes, Reverend Rogers carried with him an air of saintliness I could almost see. He made his way through the rusty gate and up to the door, and never noticed me at my perch on the roof until after he'd knocked at the door, when he looked up and started violently.

"God's mercy, boy, what are you doing up there?"

"I can see the ocean from here," I informed him. It was true. If I gazed away southward over the downs, my keen eyes could catch a line of blue in restless motion.

"Impossible," Reverend Rogers huffed. "It is too far. Anyway, should you not be at your chores?"

A reasonable question; I probably should. But I preferred to sit up there dreaming. I grinned at him, and he backed up half a step.

Fortunately, Ma came to the door then and greeted him. She seemed as shocked as I at his arrival.

"Mistress Stillskin," Reverend Rogers addressed her, "may I come in?"

Stillskin was the old couple's proper last name. And, you see, there came the magic of it, all over again. Possessing their name gave Reverend Rogers a certain power over them. It argued acquaintance, and acquaintance in turn argued intimacy. Intimacy, as I've learned, is a key that allows others to hurt you, and thus gives them magical power over you.

Quite apart from that, in our area of the world a surname often gave a hint of what a man did for a living, or what his ancestors had done. *Ford* guarded the stream. *Weaver* made cloth, *Fisher* might venture out on the tide.

Now, Pastor Rogers' use of "Stillskin" forced Ma to admit him to the cottage. He knew them, and knowing was a claim. She could scarcely turn him away.

Curiosity made me drop down from the roof and follow them inside. More than likely, I could have heard everything they said from my perch, but I could not see from there. For me, curiosity has always been a powerful force.

That's how I came to see Sir flash the sign of the horns at the good reverend, his hand down beside his knee, where he sat beside the fire.

Or perhaps, after all, he flashed it at me.

I do not think so, though, judging from the old man's expression, which soured even more than usual at the sight of Rogers.

"Good day to you, Mr. Stillskin," the good man greeted him. "A fine one it is."

"Too fine," Sir growled, "for you to darken my door."

"Will you not sit down, Reverend Rogers?" invited Ma, who possessed the only shreds of decency in that house. The poor woman looked mightily distressed, however, by this development. I could almost hear her wondering what she had on hand to offer him, and why ever he had come. "Will you take tea?"

Sir snorted, and Rogers shot him a doubtful look as he availed himself of a chair.

"No, thank you, my good woman. This will be but a brief visit."

"Thank the devil for good fortune," Sir muttered.

I almost liked him at that moment. All the blows and dire insults I'd taken from him in the past, though, prevented it.

"I've come to speak with you about the boy."

Me? No one ever focused on me. I seemed able to slip around the fringes of life precisely because no one saw me, or wanted to.

Ma pulled up a stool and eyed Reverend Rogers unhappily. "Aye, Pastor? What about him?"

Reverend Rogers looked as severe as possible for a small man who resembled a rabbit. "We have spoken of this before, Mistress Stillskin. You never registered him with the parish."

"Well," Ma began.

"Hush, Martha," Sir snapped. "I'll handle this." He shuffled forward on the bench he occupied. He inserted his pipe into his mouth and glared at Reverend Rogers over the stem. "Why would I register the boy?"

"It is customary to register all births."

"He's not my son."

Reverend Rogers glanced at Ma and cleared his throat. "I see. Still and all, Mistress Stillskin, even a child born outside of a marriage is required to be listed—"

Sir interrupted him with a loud guffaw. "Are ye addled in your wits? You think she was able to bear a child when he came along? She's been dried up long since."

Reverend Rogers' Adam's apple bobbed up and down. "Then—to whom does he belong?"

"That's the question, eh? We but took him in, and that's an end to it."

"I see," said Reverend Rogers, who clearly didn't. "But what will you do with him?"

Now there was a question. I went quite still, awaiting an answer.

"Do? *Do*?"

"You intend to continue housing him?"

Everything in the cottage went abruptly silent. For

an instant we might have been mere shadows of ourselves.

Ma's lips parted. "I wish—"

"Hush, I said, Martha."

Ma hushed.

Sir glared at me. It wasn't the sort of look he usually gave me, full of loathing and disparagement. This felt different, as if he tried to see inside me.

"We will continue giving him house room, aye, for now."

For now. What, precisely, did that mean?

"Master Stillskin, he is well grown. As a member of your household, you need to make certain provisions for him."

"I feed him, don't I? Give him a bed and clothing. Not that he earns it."

"That is just what I mean. Someday he will need to look after himself. The other children, most of them, have been to school. They've been to chapel. He has no acquaintance with either."

"He's well enough."

"Sir, he must learn a trade."

"I'll teach him all he needs to know."

At this statement, my mind reeled. Sir had taught me little, save when to duck. It was Ma who showed me how to slop the hogs, draw water from the well, even wield an axe.

For the first time, Reverend Rogers looked appalled. His nostrils pinched. "Not your trade, I hope."

"I'm a farmer. What's amiss with that?"

"You do farm, aye, but not a man from here to Land's End but knows how you truly make your living, or how you afford that poison you drink. Your name speaks your living."

Sir's eyebrows drew down. "You leave my name out o' it."

"I'm afraid I cannot. The boy should be sent to school."

"Martha will learn him."

That absurd statement made even less sense than the last. Ma stared at her husband; she could barely read and write.

Doggedly, Rogers went on, "Failing that, he needs at least to be registered in the parish records."

"I do not see why."

"Common decency, Sir."

Sir gave a grumble. Ma, effectively banned from speaking, twisted her worn hands on her apron.

Rogers pressed, "If he be a member of your household, he will have to be listed under your name."

"The hell he will." Sir pointed at me. "*That's* not mine."

Rogers flushed with ire. "I understand that, yet he has no other name, has he?"

"I call him Rum."

Again, Rogers' nostrils pinched. "No fit name for a Christian lad, and more, I think, a reflection of what usually fills that cup of yours."

The two men glared at one another.

Ma ventured, "Perhaps we could give him another name, an official one, like."

Reverend Rogers turned to her with some relief. "I think that would be a fine idea, Mrs. Stillskin."

"His name's Rum," Sir insisted.

For once in her life, Ma disregarded him. Still twisting her fingers in her apron, she said, "I've always liked the name Paul. If I'd had a son of me own, I would have called him that. Maybe Rum's official name could be Paul. 'Tis such a fine name for a man."

Her husband glared at her as if he'd never seen her before.

"His name will be Rum Paul Stillskin," she asserted, speaking it carefully, and told Reverend Rogers, "but you mark Paul Stillskin down on your church records."

He did.

Chapter Three

That visit from Reverend Rogers did not prove our last. Over the years, he returned to call on us from time to time, almost as if, along with putting my name in his register, he'd scribed us on his conscience. When the notion of our existence cropped up periodically, he'd walk out to the edge of the downs with a repeat of one request or other.

"The boy should attend school with the other children."

"The boy needs to be put to a decent trade."

One foggy autumn morning, it was, "I must insist you send the boy to chapel."

On that occasion, Sir had just returned from being out on the downs all night and was only half sober. I could have warned the good reverend it made no fit time to approach him about anything. One thing I'd learned early—schooling or no—was to keep out the way of his fists and feet when he'd taken too much to drink.

But having what even Ma called an evil streak, I listened.

Ma was careful to call me Paul when Reverend Rogers came round, the only time she did. On this morning, though, even she knew enough to button her lip.

A curse of my existence, one of many, is my

inability to forget. So I recall every detail of what happened next.

Sir sat there beside the fire with his boots still all wet and muddy from tramping, and a look on his face akin to one the devil himself might wear. Ma had left the door open behind the good reverend and the fog sort of rolled in behind him, like it wanted to grab and eat him up. To me, it looked like the evil in Sir's mind had unfurled and surrounded the pastor, so he might never escape.

When Rogers uttered his declaration, that I should go to church, Sir barked at him, "Ye've said that before."

"So I have, Mr. Stillskin, but you have not heeded me. It is far too important a matter for me to drop. The boy's soul is in peril."

"His soul," Sir repeated and started to laugh. He laughed until he wheezed, until he doubled over where he sat. "His soul, you say!"

"Aye, sir."

Suddenly, Sir sobered. "Look at him!" he cried. "Look, curse you. You think he has a soul?"

Reverend Rogers turned his eyes on me. I'd sprouted up quickly and now stood taller than Ma, which made me almost as tall as the pastor. I had little bulk with it, thin as a reed, Ma called me, however much I ate. She never cut my hair, and it hung shaggy over my ears, black as coal and with that unsettling tendency to stick out all over my head.

Rogers met my gaze for but an instant before he looked away and said, "Everyone has an immortal soul."

"You sure about that?" Sir gave Rogers no time to

reply. "Can't you see what he is?"

What am I? I wondered. I'd peered at myself in a bucket of water and knew I looked like no one else. But if Rogers knew what I was, I wished he'd tell me.

Reverend Rogers said nothing. The fog, coming in behind him—for no one had shut the door—continued to fill up the room.

Sir laughed again, a nasty sound. "Go ahead," he challenged. "Take him with you. Lead him into your chapel, see what happens then. I would not mind watching the roof cave in."

The good reverend left. After that, he did not call upon us again.

I remember when he went I followed him outside and climbed to my perch on the roof, with the fog all around me. I could hear Ma and Sir arguing inside—her voice very soft and his barking—though I couldn't catch the actual words. She asked or urged him to something; he became increasingly abusive.

I wished the fog would absorb me into it, take me away, turn me into something else even though I didn't know what I was. Ma had taught me from a very young age that everyone has a soul, that souls were part of God, and God loved everybody for that reason. If I had no soul, it followed that no one, not even God, could love me.

And no one ever would.

****

I must have been about ten at the time of Reverend Rogers' final visit. I suppose I should have been in school long since, at least part time, like the other district children who attended when they weren't kept back to help around the family farms.

Being denied an education by Sir didn't mean I never saw the other children, however, or that they didn't see me. As I say, Ma sometimes took me to the village with her on market day, to help carry her parcels. And sometimes I encountered those children while off on my own.

Indeed, one such encounter it was that let me learn what these children called me behind my back as well as to my face.

It might be said I deserved a name or two for running off and avoiding the simple chores Ma set me. She never asked much, and my help would have gone far in lightening her load. Occasionally I did help her, but far more often I'd heed the urge inside me to be away, away.

Usually, I saw the other children from a distance. One warm summer day, though, I was caught out drowsing in a little dell—very much like the palm of a shaggy hand—where, to the sound of droning bees, I'd fallen asleep.

I awoke when the first stone struck my cheek, and found myself surrounded by a ragged band of children, all staring down at me.

A rabbit, finding itself amidst a pack of foxes, could not have been more startled. Indeed, something in their expressions appeared foxlike—sharp and avid, as if the foe they'd trapped had a lame paw.

That I'd been trapped, I did not doubt. My wits could move very swiftly at times, and my sharp instincts now told me I had no escape route.

Six of them there were, ranging in size and in age from perhaps eight to twelve, four boys and two girls, all nearly as raggedy as me.

Their leader—so that razor-sharp instinct told me—was one of the older boys, tallest, with a crop of brown hair and cruel eyes.

I'd seen him before, at a distance in the village, had seen that cruel look before also and knew what it meant—the same Sir sometimes got, often when he drank.

"Look," this boy cried, "it's the damned faerie!"

The other children shifted around the edge of my dell and shuddered. *Faerie*. I could not remember hearing that word before but concluded from their reactions it must be a terrible thing.

Sir had, at various times, called me an *elf*. Ma always denied it. I knew there were other elemental creatures who populated the downs—brownies and gnomes and pixies. The word "faerie" seemed to carry darker connotations.

I half started up, got my legs under me, and shook the hair out of my eyes.

One of the girls whispered, "Look at his ears."

"Faerie," the tall boy pronounced, as if he knew everything there was to know about it. "An evil one."

The smallest boy backed off a step. The leader chastised him. "Nay, Amos, stand and look at it— remember it well. My dad says you have to recognize evil when you meet it."

Something inside me rebelled at that. Sir might deem me all manner of things, call me lazy and a no-good lout. He might conclude I had no soul, but I'd be cursed if I'd let these strangers appear from nowhere and brand me as evil.

"You don't know me," I said.

"Aye, and we don't want to," the tall boy declared.

"It's your sort come and turn the milk, make the dogs howl all night, and cause the mare to miscarry, so my dad says."

I'd never met this boy's dad and already I disliked him.

By now, I was balanced on my feet and weighing my chances of breaking free. The tall boy might be bigger than me, but life with Sir had made me tough. If I could break through their circle, I thought I could outrun them.

A big if.

"How do you know it's a faerie, George?"

"Look at it. Too tall for a pixie, too pale for a brownie, and those ears, like Agnes says. Those ears are a dead giveaway."

The other girl whispered, "Might be an elf."

Something in her voice swiveled my head so I could look at her—she stood nearly behind me. Her voice sounded beautiful, like the wind over the moor when it's feeling playful, or like one of the songs I sang to myself.

And I saw she was beautiful, with light brown hair streaked blonde by the summer sun, and gentle eyes.

But George denied it. "Nay—elves are pleasant-looking. Does that look pleasant to you, Mallie?"

Mallie. I tucked her name away in my heart.

"What should we do," the second tallest boy asked of George, "now we've caught it?"

George appeared to give that some thought. "Be careful, first of all. Faeries is full of tricks, especially the bad 'uns. I say we kill it."

He bent down and plucked a stone from the grass.

"But, George," said Mallie, "killing's a sin, so the

pastor says."

Without removing his gaze from me, George retorted, "We kill mice, don't we? Flies and lice and other vermin. Nobody goes to hell for that. This is the same thing."

Was it? I didn't feel like a mouse. Or a louse. But the others seemed convinced; they all armed themselves with stones.

All but Mallie. A glance told me she merely stood with her hands at her sides, distress apparent on her fair face.

I measured my chances again, my heart beginning to pound up in my ears. In a voice that sounded too high to be my own I said, "Let me go and I'll grant you a wish."

Most of them considered it. George stood firm. "See, I told you. That's trickery, that is."

"What kind of wish?" asked Amos.

"Anything you want."

"One for all of us, or one each?"

"One each." My throat felt tight.

"Nay," George decided for all of them, and threw his stone.

The missiles came thick and fast after that, and mostly found their marks. I don't think I noticed the pain at the time. I remained bent on getting away.

Before they did, indeed, kill me.

When George, in his enthusiasm, heaved up not a stone but a rock half as big as his head, instinct took over. I whirled and barreled up the side of the hollow directly at Mallie.

We collided, and our arms came out to clutch at one another. A new sensation rushed over me. I could smell her, like fresh grass, and feel the softness of the skin on her arms. I touched others so seldom—the need for it rose sharp like a whetted blade.

But I had to save myself.

"Let me go," I appealed to her, in a whisper.

And she whispered in return, "My wish is to see you again."

Then she stepped aside—only that.

I ran. Despite my abrasions and the bruises rising all over my body, I soon outdistanced them, though they did follow me like a pack of hounds.

I headed into the heart of Dartmoor and at length fell down behind a tuffet of tall grass, where I contemplated all he—George—had said.

Could it be true? Might I be a faerie? And what was a faerie, just?

I little knew. But I ached to find out. Maybe I could ask Ma, when we were alone and well out of Sir's hearing.

Eventually I got up and made my way home. By the time I got there, my bruises had faded and most the abrasions turned faint pink. I knew I healed quickly, but this surprised even me.

One thing I knew for certain—in George I had a new enemy, one I hated even more than Sir.

But, Mallie? Her, I did not hate.

Chapter Four

The memory of my encounter with the village children remained with me over the following months. I developed a new wariness when out by myself on the downs—very like a rabbit, in truth. I thought I would not mind meeting up with George on his own. Even though he stood taller and might make two of me in bulk, I felt pretty sure I could take him. And instinct told me that once I defeated George, the others would leave me alone.

By questioning Ma discreetly, I learned his name was actually George Goodman—a more ironically inaccurate moniker I could not imagine—and that, unfortunately, Mallie was his sister. They lived in the village where their father held the place of blacksmith. George went to school—an example, in my opinion, of why I should not attend—and also helped his father in the forge. That made it relatively easy to avoid him. He did not often have opportunity to run wild on the downs, as did I.

When I went with Ma to the market, he and I sometimes saw one another from afar. He would hiss and make the sign against evil when he laid eyes on me.

As for whether or not I had faerie blood, that too continued to haunt me. I tried asking Ma about it when we were alone, but her reaction was so strange I gained little.

"Faerie?" she repeated the first time I asked her, and her eyes widened so much I could see white all around the faded gray. "Why should ye ask that?"

"Some children said it to me. And I'm not—I'm not human, am I?"

She reddened and blessed herself, muttering something I couldn't hear.

"Eh, Ma?"

"O' course you're human. Stop with the nonsense, boy."

"How did you come by me?"

"I've told you, haven't I, how I found you?"

"How did I get there?"

But she wouldn't admit to any knowledge of that, not to my face. Instead she told me, "You're no doubt the child o' some village lass who was caught unwed."

"I don't look like anyone in the village." No one I had yet seen.

"She must have had doings with a stranger, some foreigner passing by. Someone from another land. You'll look like him."

The explanation didn't satisfy me, but neither did I wish to torment her by asking again.

Round about this time, when I would have turned twelve, Sir surprised me one morning by giving me the nod.

"Come along of me, boy."

"Eh?" I could not have heard him right. He rarely spoke directly to me, unless ordering me to some chore, and he never wanted my company. Yet there he stood in his overcoat and boots, with his cap on his head.

I glanced at Ma, who also nodded, before I took up my shabby jacket and pulled my hat down over my ears.

Outside, it pissed down rain in a grim, steady stream. Away over the downs, mist rolled like a fluffy coverlet. No fit morning to go anywhere, even for me.

"Where are we bound?" I asked. It occurred to me he might intend to lead me away from the cottage, knock me on the head, and leave me for dead. I shivered.

I should have known Sir would be much more direct than that.

He leaned toward me, and I realized we were now very nearly of a height—him but a finger or two taller. Of course, Sir was all crippled up with the rheumy joints. He must have been taller at one time.

"Rum, can you keep a secret?"

"Aye." That, at least, I knew.

"The preacher and the schoolmaster are always after me to learn you a trade. That I'm about to do."

"But we're farmers."

He snorted. "You're no farmer. You hide from chores more often than you perform 'em. And this bit o' farm's so poor, we'd have starved long since."

"Oh."

"Come along, now, and I'll show you how I really earn my bread."

"Why?"

He glared at me.

"You've never wanted to learn me anything before."

He spat into the heath. "I been thinking. If something happens to me, you'll need to keep Martha fed."

"Nothing's going to happen to you." He seemed as

indestructible as the downs themselves, like a rock or a pillar of stone.

"Even so."

He led the way off into the mist, and I followed. It was a bad morning for trying to determine direction, yet I knew I'd be able to find the way again—over hillock, and around tor. My senses were just that good.

At last, a menhir loomed at us out of the mist, three stones together, one balanced atop the other two. A magical place. I could feel the power flowing from it to dance along my skin and knew it meant something to me. But Sir ignored the stones as if they did not exist.

Not far away was a dell like those that populated the downs. Sir shuffled down into it and started pulling at a pile of dried heather stacked at the bottom. A neat row of small casks came into view, a pile of firewood, and a strange contraption the like of which I'd never seen.

"There now," said Sir. "That's what's been feeding you all your life."

"What is it?"

"Think. Martha says you're quick. How quick?"

I opened my mind the way I sometimes did when I wanted something to happen or not happen. Nothing came, so I sniffed. "There's liquor in that."

"Aye. Yon's a still. It's how I got my name, and my forefathers ahead o' me."

"A still." I'd never heard the word. "It makes whiskey."

"It makes rotgut."

"The stuff you drink?"

He grunted. "Here." He snatched a small jug from the bottom of the dell, uncorked it, and handed it to me.

I drank.

It was my first taste of spirits, and a bad introduction. The stuff ran down my throat in a trail of fire, rough as lye. I coughed and coughed.

Sir laughed. "I don't drink that," he told me, his tone implying I was very stupid indeed. "I trade it for the good rum I do drink."

My eyes streaming, I managed to say, "Trade, to who?"

"That will be made clear in time. For now, you need only remember where this is, so you can find it again when we bring the cart. You build a fire beneath that big kettle, see? Just like on Martha's hearth. Then you cook the mash and draw off the liquid. It goes in the kegs to age—not long. Then we hauls it to the coast, where we hides it for pick-up. See?"

Dimly, I saw. "And no one knows?"

"Not even Martha, though I don't doubt she suspects. The fellow who comes to pick it up and brings me rum in exchange is the only one. And now, you." Sir's pale eyes regarded me with frightening intensity. "I do not need to say what will happen to you if you tell."

"No, Sir." I swallowed. "I won't tell."

In the months that followed, Sir taught me all the details of the process. I learned how to fire the still on foggy days that wouldn't reveal the smoke and how to haul the cart, like a draft horse, for we had none. I met the man—his sole name Joe—who came to collect the stuff from a cave where Sir stashed it, and gleaned the information that he took it across the channel to France.

I never received a penny for my work, nor so much as a single draught of rum. But Sir did reiterate several times that I owed him and must keep up the running so to provide for Ma, if he couldn't.

I suppose that meant he cared about her, in his way. Which in turn, I reckoned, meant—much to my surprise—he was actually capable of love.

Chapter Five

What with helping Sir tend his illicit business and the few chores Ma succeeded in persuading me to perform, I had less time to myself on the downs. I made the most of the time I could grab, though, being happiest when on my own—or so I thought then.

I cannot, in truth, tell where the hours and days went when I lay in some dell, safe away from the rest of the world, listening to the bees hum or dodging raindrops. Truly, time melted away, and I merely absorbed the feeling of rightness, as if I belonged somewhere at last. I made myself a fife from a hollow reed and often sang songs that came to me. Even to my own ears, my voice sounded like bird song, only sweeter and purer. Contentment found me then, the only ease I truly knew.

By the time I was fourteen, I stopped growing. I was just a bit proud of Sir's wizened height then, much smaller than the village boys who had, as I saw from a distance, outstripped me. But I possessed prodigious strength, despite my weedy-looking limbs, and was very quick indeed. I'd learned I could *wish*—a term I used because I possessed no other for it. I might wish myself so still, not even a rabbit would see me, wish myself out of Sir's sight. I could wish things to happen, like making someone trip over his own feet at the market. But in order for that to happen, I had to be in the right state of mind. I had to be totally *me,* if that makes any sense. And that usually only happened out on the downs.

Then one day I got caught. Truly caught. Only…maybe it was actually the fulfillment of somebody else's wish.

It was a sunny day in midsummer, and I was going on fifteen. I'd slipped away in order to avoid the haying, and lay on my back in my favorite dell, watching the birds fly overhead.

From time to time, I called to them by echoing their whistles. When I did, they might come and perch on the gorse bushes at the rim of my dell and look at me. Discerning I wasn't in fact a bird, they'd fly off again.

I must have dozed after a while, for I dreamed. There was a song in the dream, and a word which I heard clear—*calling.* A calling song, I thought when I woke, and began singing it to the sky.

It didn't take long before someone came to the rim of the dell and, just like the birds, peered down at me. A face like a flower she had, all pink and white, with lips like soft rose petals and eyes like pieces of the sky.

I knew her, of course. I'd seen her around the village with the rest of her family, including her brother who'd now grown into a hulking lad, nearly as big as their father, the smith. We'd never spoken, she and I, since that first day.

Now she smiled. So did I. As if she'd done it a thousand times, she slid down into the dell on her fanny. The sky closed over us.

She said, "Hello. I'm so glad I found you. I wanted very much to see you again."

And I replied, "Aye, that was your wish."

"You remember?"

"Of course I do." I pushed myself up onto my elbows, wondering if my dream really had ended or if I dreamed still.

"My name's Mallie Goodman. It's a funny first name, innit? My ma called me Mallow, but she only uses that when she's angry with me."

I inspected her face from brow to chin and asked, "Who could ever be angry with you?"

She flushed a little. "You'd be surprised. There are six of us, and she loses patience regular. You're an only, eh?"

"What?" I couldn't believe I sat there conversing with her, in my dell.

"An only child." She sighed. "I can't even imagine it. Seems someone's always griping or chatting at our house. That's why I like it out here. It's quiet."

An only. Surely she knew I didn't really belong to Ma and Sir. Should I say?

She inspected me in turn, starting at my toes and working upward. When she reached my face, a new expression invaded her eyes, one I didn't quite comprehend, yet which brought the heat to my skin.

"Your name's Rum, right?"

For some reason, I said, "That's just what Sir calls me—Rum. Ma calls me Paul. Rum Paul."

"Who's Sir?"

"That's—Ma's old man. Her husband."

"But he's not related to you?"

Carefully I confessed, "I'm not related to either of them. Not by blood." Blood was important, in this part of the world. People could recite a list of their ancestors back many generations.

She smiled again. How can I describe one of Mallie's smiles? Sweet and beguiling, warm and intimate. I'd never before received anything like.

"Rum Paul, I like that. It sounds sort of—magical." Before I could comment, she hurried on. "I heard you singing. That was you, wasn't it?"

"Aye."

"It was one of the most beautiful things ever, like birdsong and water rushing, and the wind over the downs when it first lifts up and starts to hum, after the quiet." She hesitated and asked shyly, "Will you sing for me again?"

Sing for her. Give her the innermost part of myself, what I kept private away from the world, where I dwelt?

Ah, but wouldn't I give anything in trade for her company?

I asked, "Aren't you afraid of me?"

"Should I be?"

"Nay."

She held up her hands, as if giving a shrug, as if offering herself to me. "Then I'm not."

"In the village, folk must say a lot of things about me."

"The village," she said sweepingly, "is seldom quiet, and folk say a lot, aye, but most of it means nothing. 'Tis as if—as if they need to be gossiping, aye? To lift them out of their own dull lives."

"Oh."

"So you should not take it too personal."

I wanted to say it was hard not to take it personally when the insults and the stones came flying, but I didn't. She was here, sitting in my dell, not an arm's reach from me. And nothing else much mattered.

"Rum Paul," she requested formally, "will you sing for me?"

I sang. At first my voice sounded husky, rough with uncertainty, but it soon cleared out and became true. I sang the old songs and some I'd made new. I tweeted for her, I trilled, I crooned.

She slid down on her back with her arms folded behind her head, for a pillow, and listened. At first she closed her eyes. A look of bliss came over her face, and she smiled. At length her eyes came open to rest on my face, two pieces of the sky regarding me.

When the last song evaporated into the warm air, she said, "It's just like heaven, isn't it? Rum Paul, do you believe that our souls go somewhere beautiful when we die?"

"No."

"Reverend Rogers says it's so. If my soul could go anywhere after I die, I would want it to be here—with you, like, listening. There couldn't be anything better."

Maybe I fell in love with Mallie at that moment. Maybe I'd already been in love with her from our first encounter, when she whispered in my ear. Maybe I'd been looking all the while, my whole life long, for someone to whom I could give my heart. To prove that, like Sir, I truly had one.

Whatever the case, I gave it to her then, wholly and completely. For all time. It hurt, in the giving. But it felt so wonderful I couldn't speak.

It seemed I didn't need to; she sat up and faced me. We gazed into each other's eyes.

What did I see, in that field of blue? Liking and

acceptance, understanding and kindness. What did she see?

Did she see I had a soul?

"Thank you, Rum Paul. You've given me the most perfect afternoon. May I come and visit you again?"

My throat felt so tight I could barely speak. I wanted to touch her, more than I'd ever wanted anything. I didn't dare.

I nodded.

"How will I know you're here?" she asked.

"I—I'll send you a thought. A *wish*."

"You can do that?" She tipped her head, lips parted in amazement.

"Aye." For her, I could do anything.

"That's magic, that is. I knew you were magic."

"Aye." For her, I wanted to gather all the magic that shimmered in the air around me, cup it in my hands, hold it out like a gift. "But don't tell anyone."

She shook her head. "Our secret." She got to her feet, a slight girl so full of beauty it astounded me she could contain it all. "I have to go. I'll get a thrashing as it is."

Everything inside me rebelled. I might receive any number of thrashings; no one should touch her in anger.

She stilled at what she saw in my eyes. "Don't look that way. It's all right. Pa don't mean anything by it."

She stepped up onto the turf at the top of the dell and balanced there a moment before hopping back down and planting a kiss on my cheek.

"Never mind," she said. "Don't worry."

She leapt back up out of the dell and ran.

Chapter Six

For the next three years, Mallie Goodman and I met out on the downs. In all weathers—sun, rain, frost, and snow—we kept our hidden trysts and no one ever knew.

We divided the meetings among varied places so we wouldn't get caught. There were any number of dells, standing stones, even an old shepherd's hut. I would send her a wish and we would wait, one for the other, until we could be together. Sometimes I did not need to send a wish—she merely came because she needed me.

I lived for those meetings. In between, I helped Sir with his still, taking over more and more of the heavier duties. I pulled the cart on my own and often went to meet Joe on my own, also. He would show up in a small boat, and we would load the rotgut from the cave; he'd pay me in bottles of rum and sometimes coin, or a combination of both.

I never grew to like Sir any better for spending more time with him, and he never liked me. He insulted me roundly and often, cursed me out and damned me for being lazy and worthless. For the most part, I ignored him. I was even quicker now, though I never got any bigger, and could mostly dodge the blows he aimed at me.

I did not change, except to fill out a wee bit and

sprout a beard on my chin. But Mallie grew ever more beautiful. When we saw one another in the village—and had to pretend we didn't—I noticed how the other lads' heads turned as she passed by. I hated that, but I could not blame them.

Our relationship had, by then, surpassed the bounds of friendship, though we'd done nothing more than hold hands and kiss. My need for her encompassed the physical, but went far beyond it. My one companion, my one comfort, Mallie made up my world.

She was the only person who made me laugh. She could be very mischievous and silly, and she made me silly in turn. I loved being silly and clever and outrageous. I loved the way she looked at me.

Then one day in autumn—I must have been nearly eighteen and she sixteen or seventeen—she sent me a wish. It found me, sharp and urgent, while I worked at forking over the last of the potato mounds, a job Sir had been after me to do for days.

As soon as I heard Mallie's call in my mind, I threw down the fork and hied out of there. Sir came out of the cottage door.

"Rum! Where d'ye think ye're going?" And when I gave him a glare, he continued, "Finish your work, ye worthless lump."

Ignoring him, I ran. By now I think Mallie and I could have found one another on the downs in utter darkness. I knew she ran to me as I ran to her, and I knew where.

I got there first and, out of habit, ducked down into the dell, now brown with dying scrub grass.

Something was wrong. I could feel Mallie's distress coming at me like an injured bird on the wing.

It made me feel edgy and helpless.

She arrived mere moments later, breathless also and flushed in the face. She slid down into our hollow as always, and I made room for her beside me.

"Mallie, what's wrong?"

"Oh, Rum Paul. Oh, Rum Paul."

"What—?"

She started to cry. I'd never before seen Mallie weep, never imagined such a thing, and it knocked me back on my heels. Was she ill? Dying? People did die, I knew.

I could not live without her.

"Mallie?" I seized her hand. "Tell me."

"I don't know how." She palmed the tears from her cheeks, and I trembled anew. Some terrible thing, this was.

"Just say it."

"Very well. Jules Longford spoke to my father today."

Baffled, I shook my head. "What's a Jules Longford?"

"Not what, silly—who. He lives on the other side of the village. His pa runs a carting business. My pa says it would be a good match."

She might have been speaking a foreign tongue for all the sense it made to me.

"I don't understand."

She swiped her cheeks again with the hand not clasped in mine. "He wants to pay me suit."

"Suit?"

"To court me. To marry me. Don't you remember that story we read?"

Here in the dell, or in one of our other meeting

places, she'd taught me to read. She would bring tattered books from home—just a few—and together we'd read stories. One of them involved a young man courting a young woman in view of marriage. Things had not gone well for them, after.

"Aye, I remember." I didn't forget much. But I'd never imagined Mallie marrying, and the idea turned my stomach. "Tell him no."

"Simple as that, is it?"

"Aye."

"Rum Paul, girls wed. There's naught else to be done, and Pa will expect it."

"Do you want to wed?"

"Not him. But Pa—like I said—thinks it's a good match. Jules will have his father's business someday. He will be able to provide for me."

"Not him. You said you don't want to marry him. But you do want to marry?"

"Aye."

"Who?"

"Surely you can guess."

She gazed into my eyes and I into hers. During those moments, the world went away, I swear it did. There was only her love, like all the magic that had ever found me, like every wish rolled into one.

"Oh, Mallie," I whispered then. "Oh, sweet powers of the heavens and earth, what have I to offer you?"

She wound her arms around my neck. "The magic in your smile. The laughter in your eyes. So much beauty, when you sing, that sometimes my heart rises right up like it can fly."

"But that—by Jove's beard, Mallie, that's not a living. I could never support you." A truth about which

I'd never before cared, but which now turned me sick inside.

"Will you not have Sir's farm after he's gone?"

"I doubt it."

"But to whom else will he leave it? There's no one."

For the first time ever, surprisingly, I thought about that. I thought Sir would rather strangle on his own tongue than leave me anything.

Mallie urged, "Why would he train you in his trade—though you won't tell me what it is—if he didn't consider you his son?"

"I don't think—"

"Rum Paul..." She tightened her embrace. "Why don't you talk to him?"

"Talk to Sir?"

"If he means to leave you his farm, maybe you could offer for me, and then I wouldn't have to consider Jules."

I nearly laughed aloud. "Me, offer for you?"

"Aye. I know you love me."

I knew it too, the way I knew the blood ran in my veins, and air filled my lungs. But I shook my head. "What do you suppose your father would say to that? And your brother?"

"I don't know. But neither do I see how I can take any other man to husband, feeling the way I do for you."

She began to weep again, rain falling from a clear blue sky.

"Hush," I told her. "Hush. I love you, Mallie, indeed I do, and you're breaking my heart."

I pulled her very gently into my arms. We held

each other so for a long while, heartbeats mingling.

She breathed, "What are we to do?"

"Stall him. Your pa—can't you put him off, somehow?"

"What use is that?"

"Maybe this Jules will get tired of waiting and marry someone else."

"Aye, maybe."

"If not—" I broke off. If not, I might seek out Jules Longford and kill him. I could move very quietly when I chose; I could eliminate him from our world.

"Rum Paul, why won't you offer for me?"

"You've heard the things your brother says about me, Mallie."

"That you're not human." Strangely, this subject came up but seldom between us. In all our hours together, she'd rarely raised it, and I'd come to think it didn't matter, not to her. But what lacked importance here, in our private world, would matter very much indeed were I to take the nearly unimaginable step of approaching her father.

Now she asked, "Don't you have any idea who your people were?"

Holding her in my arms, I gave her the truth. "Not a hint. Ma thinks my father was a foreigner from some far-off land—maybe a sailor."

"And your ma?"

"I don't know," I repeated. "She dropped me in Ma's garden." I held Mallie away from me, far enough so I could look into her eyes. "You know, and I know, one of them weren't human. I don't look like other folks. I didn't grow the same. Look at my ears, my arms and legs—my eyes. Have you ever seen a human like me?"

She bit her lip and shook her head. "But, Rum Paul, you make me happy, like no one else. When you smile at me, when you tease me, when you make up songs for me—oh, that's best of all."

I shook her gently. "Your pa will never allow it."

"Then we'll run off together."

"And live where?"

"On the downs. Here, like two wild creatures. You're already half wild anyway."

"And if little 'uns should come along?"

"We'll raise them wild, too."

"Ah, Mallie, you have no idea."

She kissed me. So sweet was it, I couldn't help but kiss her back.

"Ah," I told her when the sweetness ebbed, and her lips left mine, "stall them, the best you can."

Chapter Seven

Winter came, blowing down fast and hard from Wales, spitting snow and freezing the ground as hard as iron.

Ma took a chill while out tending the beasts. Sir blamed me for it—said I should be doing the chores for her, and her in by the warm fireside.

In that, he was right. Ma had been good to me my whole life long, and I owed her. But the habit of shirking my duties was by then ingrained, and Mallie and I were still meeting out on the downs.

Her father continued to press her hard about hearing Jules Longford's suit, as she called it, though I couldn't figure what a set of clothes had to do with marriage.

She continued to resist, though she said her brother George, who thought highly of Langford, told her she was a fool to refuse him. Sometimes she came to me with unexplained bruises on her cheek and jaw. I think George struck her, though she never said.

Maybe that was because she knew—she knew that if they ever truly harmed her, I'd hunt them down the way a wolf hunts a vole, and tear them limb from limb.

One winter's day we stayed out late together, in the ruined shepherd's hut. It was cold, but I'd found if I held out my hands, half cupped together, I could make a bit of warmth, and if we huddled together very close, it served.

I'd made a new song and wanted to sing it for her. It was about holly, and how the spirit of the tree came to life when the other greenery died. It spoke of red berries, snow crunching underfoot, and breath like smoke. It spoke of endurance in the face of want.

When the dark began to filter into the hut, we kissed and made to go our separate ways home. As always when we parted, Mallie gazed into my eyes and said, "I love you, Rum Paul Stillskin."

"I love you, Mallie Goodman."

"Forever?"

"Forever."

"Then I can sleep happy this night."

When I reached home, the new dark had come down. Yellow lamplight glowed through the windows of the cottage. Before lifting the latch, something made me pause and look in.

The cottage had but two rooms, besides the loft in which I slept—the big room where we sat and ate, both, and the small alcove where Ma and Sir slept. Since she fell ill, Ma had been bedded in the cot in the main room, near the fire.

Looking in, I saw a shocking sight: Ma, lying there on the cot, and Sir perched beside it, with his hand on her brow.

I'd never before seen him treat her with anything approaching tenderness, and it momentarily froze me where I stood.

When I lifted the latch and went in, Sir turned on me. "Where in hell have you been?"

"Out."

"Runnin' the downs, like the fey thing you are?

Well, you can do some more runnin'. Go and fetch the doctor."

"Where?"

"Little Underhill."

"That's over ten mile."

"Then you'd better get going."

I looked at Ma. "What's wrong with her?"

"She's dyin'. Hurry."

I hurried. I could run fast when I wanted, but ten miles in the cold made a stretch even for me. All the while, I kept sending out wishes: *Don't let her die. Don't let her die*. I never knew what Ma meant to me, till then. She was one of only two people in all the world who cared about me.

I fetched the doctor. It took a while even after I got to Little Underhill because I didn't know where he lived. Once I knocked him up, he had to hitch his cart to a fussy brown nag.

We were almost too late.

Ma was still alive when we got there, but barely. She was breathing raspy breaths, struggling for them, and wheezing.

The doctor went to examine her. Sir never said a word to me. The doctor came over to where we stood and said, "Her lungs are enflamed, and she's very weak. Nothing to be done, I'm afraid."

"No," I whispered.

Somehow, Ma heard me. She opened her eyes and held out her hand. I went and knelt beside the cot.

She looked so small, there under the blanket. So frail. But she clasped my fingers hard in hers.

Her faded gray eyes looked at me intently. She could barely speak, and I had to lean close when she said, "I always loved you."

The breath rattled in her chest and stopped.

The doctor came and lifted me away from her. I don't remember much after that, just flashes of pictures. Some women came, neighbors, and cared for Ma's corpse while I waited in the byre. Truth be told, I slept in the byre that night. I didn't want to go back into the cottage where she lay.

I remember the next morning I did go in and saw her all dressed up, looking far fancier than she ever did in life. Sir came and ordered me to do the chores.

I did them.

A day or two later, there was a funeral service, and Ma went into the cold ground. I'd never imagined feeling so abandoned.

We came home to a chilly, empty cottage afterward—cold not only because the fire had burned down.

We were barely in the door before Sir, also dressed in his best clothing, turned to me and said, "Get out."

"What?"

"You heard me. Damn bastard. I only ever kept you for her sake."

My mind reeled. I certainly didn't relish the prospect of living here alone with him, but I'd just lost Ma. How could I lose the only home I'd ever known?

"But," I stammered, "but you trained me, showed me the still and the cave."

"That was only for her sake, so you could take care o' her if something happened to me first." He bared his teeth. "That's not goin' to happen now, is it?"

"Where will I go?" I didn't want to ask that question; it came on its own.

He waved an arm. "Out. On them downs where you always wanted to be, you unnatural creature. She was good to you, and how did you repay her? You killed her, that's how."

"I didn't."

"You did!" He roared it. "If you'd been here doing for her as she asked, she'd never have been out in all weathers, caring for the beasts. She'd never have caught that chill."

It didn't occur to me to say that if he'd ever lifted a finger 'round the farm she might still be with us also. What he said hurt too much. It hurt because it was true.

"Get your things and go," he repeated, and added with some satisfaction, "I been waitin' near twenty years to say that."

Anger came to my rescue then, along with hatred for him. I went to the loft, where I discovered I didn't own much, just some ragged clothes, some pretty stones, and my reed pipe. A small coin or two Joe had given me when I did jobs. I took it all but the stones. There were thousands of stones on the downs.

Sir never said another word to me, nothing when I left. He sat there in his usual place beside the hearth with his pipe in his mouth and didn't so much as look at me.

I fled, as he'd suggested, to the downs. The atmosphere of the cottage had already changed, become unwelcoming. But the weather that night proved equally inhospitable. Full dark had come down by then, and it spat a combination of sleet and rain. The wind, as I recall, blew in raggedy gusts and buffeted me as I went, more or less blindly, into the night.

I came, mainly by instinct, to one of my hidey-holes, one of those Mallie and I shared. There I hunkered down like an animal and tried to comprehend what had happened to my life.

All gone so quickly. I wanted to go back and hurt Sir the way he'd just hurt me. I knew I could sneak into the cottage silently enough that he wouldn't know I was there. I pictured his face if he woke up and saw me standing over him like vengeance itself.

But I didn't think Ma would want that, not so soon anyway—not on her burial day. Out of belated respect for her, I stayed where I was. I didn't cry, though I felt like it. I rarely cried tears, and in this case, it wouldn't help. I didn't call to Mallie, either. I'd caught a glimpse of her at the churchyard, but only from a distance—her family would have no reason to let her attend Martha Stillskin's service. Now I let no wish escape my mind, for the night was dark and the weather foul.

And much as I wanted to see her, I made no fit company.

Chapter Eight

Perhaps I should have renounced Sir's last name then—Stillskin. For in truth it was none of my own and he had cast me off. Had I done, none of the rest of it might have happened, for as it proved out, the danger lay in the name as much as anywhere.

Mallie found me the next day. My desire must have escaped me despite all my efforts, for she came right to the place where I hid, even though the weather continued foul.

She brought food, which I'd already discovered to be my biggest lack. Other things I might do without, but I'd become accustomed to eating regularly.

She slid down into the hollow beside me and stared at me earnestly.

"Why are you here, Rum Paul, and not safe at home?"

When I explained the whole of it to her, her eyes widened in distress. "But what will you do?"

"Live here on the downs, as he bade me."

"All alone? Winter is long and hard. How can you survive?"

"I'll manage. I feel more at home here than anywhere else."

"Aye, but—spring is a long way off, Rum Paul. You'll need fuel and food. I cannot always bring it to you."

"I know."

"Perhaps you could go back, make amends with him."

"I'll be damned if I will." Quite possibly, I'd been born damned.

"You have rights to that farm."

I lifted my head and looked her full in the eyes. "I don't. I don't belong to him. I never did."

"Still—"

"If I go back there, Mallie," I burst out, "it will be to hurt him. Do you want that?"

"No, Rum Paul." She touched my hair, and some of my ire drained away. "It's just that, without the farm, my pa will never countenance us getting married."

I told her, because I'd been facing truths all night, "He wouldn't anyway."

I felt the protest rise up inside her at that, protest and dismay. It turned me sick inside. I could feel her worry too, and knew she was thinking the specter of Jules had just got brighter.

But she voiced none of that and merely put out her arms and embraced me. We sat like that a long while, her holding me like a child with my cheek against her breast, and her murmuring all the while.

Some of my pain eased, at least temporarily. But she couldn't stay with me forever.

At last she stirred. "My love, I must go."

My love. Only one person left in the world now loved me.

She must have sensed my reluctance for her to leave, because she said, "If I am away too long, 'twill make it more difficult for me to come again."

"Aye."

"Rum Paul, you cannot stay here. You'll have to find some place better. The shepherd's hut, maybe."

"Maybe."

"Will you go there?" She touched my cheek tenderly. "Do you promise?"

"That's farther for you to come."

"I don't mind."

"'Twill make it harder for you."

Something kindled in the endless blue of her eyes. "That doesn't matter. I'd go any distance to be with you, Rum Paul Stillskin. Cross any gulf or chasm. No matter what separates us, I will always return to you. Do you understand?"

My lips trembled. "That sounds like a vow."

"It is a vow." She kissed me, halting the trembling and warming me right through. "Call me if you need me."

"Thank you, Mallie. I…" I had no words, so I drew her close and kissed her again. When that kiss ended, she smiled at me.

"I love you so much," she said.

"And I you. You have no notion how much."

"I will try and come tomorrow. If I can't—"

"I understand. Let me see you part way home."

"All right."

We went hand in hand through the gusty wind and swirling sleet, and parted well out of sight from the village. When she went, all warmth went with her.

****

For two days, Mallie did not return. The food she'd brought soon gave out, and hunger rode me hard, the need for her still harder. The cold proved difficult also.

At last the weather eased. A watery sun emerged,

and Mallie came with it, over the downs dusted with white, her cheeks flushed pink.

She found me out in the open, seeking to warm myself in the weak sun. I'd tried my trick of emitting warmth to fill the hut, and discovered it worked only until my energy began to wane. After that, I got cold clear through.

Mallie ran the last of the distance and threw herself into my arms. "Oh, I'm so glad to see you. Are you all right? I'm that sorry I couldn't come. You must be starved, but no matter now. I brought food."

"Why didn't you come sooner?" I asked when we sat side by side, and I consumed some of what she'd brought.

"Pa insisted there was no reason for me to go out in such weather. I didn't want to make him suspicious by insisting."

"No."

"But I missed you ever so much."

"And I you." She had no idea. "Is there any talk in the village about me leaving the farm?"

She shook her head. "I don't suppose anyone knows, what with Sir's cottage being outlying and all. Have you given any more thought to what you'll do?"

"Aye." That I had.

Mallie lifted her brows at me.

"I want to get back at him." My thoughts had not improved over the past two days.

"Oh, no, Rum Paul. Revenge is unworthy of you."

That I knew it was not.

"'Tis a sin."

"I am a sin," I retorted viciously.

"You are no such thing! You're good and beautiful,

made up of strength and magic, just like the downs. You're…" She seemed to search for a word. "You're elemental."

"I'm what?"

"Reverend Rogers talks about that in chapel sometimes. How God's in charge of the elements, both those outside us, like the sea and the wind, and those inside. When he said it, I thought, God might be in charge of those things, but my Rum Paul's made up of them."

Her Rum Paul.

"I've got naught in common with Reverend Rogers' god."

"No."

"If Sir's to get what he deserves, there's only me to serve it to him."

"Aye, but Rum Paul, it could set off all kinds of trouble."

It could. I'd been thinking about that, too. I'd need to be careful. "I just intend to pay him a visit."

"And ask if you can go back there?"

I hated to lie to her. I hated worrying her, even more. "Something like that."

"Well, all right then. Rum Paul, I can't stay long. Walk me back again?"

We walked hand in hand, through the sunshine this time, and when we kissed I could feel her concern for me.

"Promise you'll be very careful, and you'll not do anything foolish."

"Foolish is a matter of opinion."

"Rum Paul—"

"I will be careful."

"Good." She embraced me hard. "You're so precious to me."

I'd never been that, to anyone. My own ma—whoever she was—had abandoned me in Ma's garden.

The next day it rained hard. I stayed inside the hut, where I had a chance of keeping dry. That night, I went to the farm, just to see if I could do it and not get caught. I peered in the window at Sir, who drowsed by the fire, all snug and warm. He had his flask of rum close to hand and was likely drunk.

I could slip inside now, if I chose, and finish him. I'm not sure what stopped me, save I was still considering my options.

I spent the balance of that night in the byre with the animals, nice and warm, but left before first light, with an empty stomach.

From a distant rise, I watched Sir emerge from the cottage, take up the cart, and tow it off toward his stash. I did go inside then, looking for food. There wasn't much in the house, but I ate his bread and a bit of meat I found, and stole some cheese for later.

Perhaps he'd think the mice took it.

Then, out of sheer mischief, I hid his flask and another wee cask of rum he kept. I thought about setting fire to the place—let him be as homeless as me—but decided if I ended up firing the cottage, I wanted it to be while he was inside.

To finish, I stole a hammer, some nails and a few planks from the byre. I hated picking up the nails—the touch of pure iron always made me feel sick—but I put them in a cloth bag so they wouldn't meet my skin.

All the way back to the hut, I thought about my choices, for I did have some. I could sneak into the cottage and murder Sir in cold blood. Part of me wanted very badly to do that, but I didn't know what Mallie would think of me if she found out.

I could fire the cottage and let him die in the flames, then take over his business. I thought Joe would deal with me in Sir's stead. That way, I'd have the farm plus a living.

Or—and part of me also liked this option—I could betray Sir to the excise men, for smuggling. The king's agents were forever scouring the coast for such illegal activities. Sir and Joe had both warned me to watch out for them.

If I turned Sir in, and he received the king's punishment, he'd suffer far longer than a few agonizing moments in a fire. And I'd still have the cottage. But it would be impersonal, that. Maybe far too impersonal.

I wanted to see him squirm.

Chapter Nine

Before I could make up my mind how to serve Sir his just deserts, the weather turned again. By then, I'd made some repairs to the old hut and got the chimney drawing, though fuel proved scarce.

Mallie came only seldom. It was a long walk to the hut from her house in the village, and difficult for her to get away. I tried to be understanding, but I felt desperate for her company.

When she did come, the time together passed so blissfully, I spared barely a thought for Sir. I sang for her, made up stories, and performed small magical tricks. No matter what else I lacked, her presence made everything right in my world.

I had to ask her, though, for news from the village; she rarely told me unless I did. Not much happened there, so she insisted when I did ask. Her brother George courted Betsy Palmer from Little Underhill. She figured they'd marry in the spring.

She rarely mentioned Jules Longford. At last I asked her outright.

"Is Longford still paying you attention?"

She nodded, and refused to look at me. I felt my heart seize momentarily, a lump of coal in my chest.

"He been coming 'round a lot?"

"Aye. Pa's even spoken to him about my dowry."

"What's that?"

"My marriage portion. Pa earns a fair living as blacksmith, and he's set a bit aside. My husband will get that, when we wed."

I grunted. "Does Longford want you or this portion?"

She did look at me then. "Both."

"You're already mine."

"I know, Rum Paul. I am, forever, here in my heart. But I'm afraid some things might come between."

"They've been working on you, haven't they? Wearing you down."

Her eyes filled with tears. "It's so hard."

I pictured her there alone with them, surrounded as if by a pack of snapping foxes. I took both her hands in mine. "You have to stay strong."

"Aye."

"We belong together, you and me."

"I know. But how? And when? Pa won't wait forever."

"Till the spring. I'll think of something by spring."

She gazed into my eyes. "All right. I'll hang on till then. Now hold me. And sing to me."

I did.

****

I planned hard after that, planned smart, at least so I thought. I understood I had no chance of winning Mallie if I had nothing. Truth was, I had no chance of winning her anyway, being who—and what—I was. But it would be the height of foolishness to burn down the cottage, reducing the value of the farm, if I meant to try. So despite how I hated Sir, I couldn't roast him in his bed.

No. I had to fix it so I got the farm and could

continue running the rotgut on the side. So I couldn't turn him in, either, because there went the business.

Seemed to me that left only one option. I had to serve him as he deserved and make it look like either a natural death or an accident.

I took to haunting the farm and came up with a scheme, but then the weather worsened in earnest. That winter was as cold a one as I'd ever seen on the downs. The ground turned to iron, and the sky seemed to be always spitting something—icy rain, sleet, or snow.

I told Mallie not to come so far across the moor—you have to believe I did. Much as I wanted—ached—to see her, I knew it was too hard a journey for her there and back, in such weather.

"Keep away," I bade her during one visit, "and I'll come to your place instead. Ain't there a big shed out back of the forge? We can meet there."

Still fighting for breath after her walk, she shook her head. "Nay, Rum Paul. George goes out there for supplies, regular. If he should see you…" She shivered.

So I let it ride, fool that I was.

And then came the day—and an ugly day it was, spewing hail and rain—when she arrived looking sweaty and feverish, and near collapsed in my arms.

"Mallie, you're ill. You should never have come all this way."

"I had to. I wanted so badly to see you."

"You're wet clear through. Come sit beside the fire." I built it up, using a small jolt of magic.

"Nay, Rum Paul, just hold me. Please."

I did, but she was wracked by chills and waves of fever in turns. She'd brought me food, one of the main reasons she always came, for she hadn't been out in four days due to the weather. I heated some of the broth and fed it to her. Her throat, she said, felt too sore to let her swallow.

I'll admit fear gripped me then. What to do? I wanted to keep her there with me but knew if she didn't come home there'd be a great hue and cry. I didn't think she'd make it home on her own.

I felt distraught and guilty that she'd come out on my behalf, risking her health. I hadn't done enough for Ma, and she'd died. Now, Mallie.

I kept her there till she warmed through and her clothing dried, holding her in my arms the while, where she burned and thrashed. Then I bundled her as best I could, wrapped her, and carried her home.

I knew, because she'd impressed it upon me, how dangerous it was for us to be spied together. And the distance I carried her was far, but my physical strength stood me in good stead. I sheltered her from as much of the pelting rain as I could and, when we neared the village, pulled my hood well up over my head.

At her door, I set her down and, quivering in every limb, knocked at the door.

I think it was one of her sisters who answered. She stared, and her face contorted in horror—not at me, not then, but at Mallie's state.

"By heaven! What—?" She switched her gaze to me. "Who are you?"

"She's ill. Take care of her," I growled, and was gone as if I'd never been there.

I fled away home by a circuitous route, just in case anyone followed. Full dark had fallen when I reached the hut. No one came after me.

No one.

Worry? Let me tell you, no one ever worried as I did then. Not knowing is a torment, a beast with sharp claws. She might have recovered and been on the road to feeling herself again. She might have been at death's door, this one person who, to me, meant everything.

One day passed, then two. Then I felt her *wishing*.

I awoke in the morning from a fitful doze to the pull of it. Mallie, the other half of my being, of my very life, wished for me.

Breathless wonder filled me then. It meant she was alive, the most important thing. Alive and focused on me.

Longing for me. The more attention I gave to the sensation, the clearer the wish became. Raw, desperate need it was, weak and yet so strong it made a demand of me.

I ask you, how could I resist that call? For all that happened after, how could I have done anything but go to her when she pulled at me that way?

Indeed, I heeded nothing else—not the weather, which remained vile, not my own hunger, or the danger to me inherent in going back to the village in broad daylight. So bright did her need for me sound in my heart, it narrowed my very world.

To one thing—Mallie.

"I am coming, I am coming," I muttered as I donned my coat and found my boots and shut the door of the hut behind me.

A long distance it was, over the downs. This land I loved—land of my birth—lay gray with hoarfrost, all the rough bushes frozen in agonized contortions. The wind moaned over it like a living thing. I wished then I could ride the wind. But I didn't know how, and my feet had to serve.

With her desire clanging in my head, I ran most the distance. The wind streamed my hair out behind me and ice collected on my cheeks and eyelashes, but I never paused.

At the outskirts of the village, I once more drew the hood over my head and tugged it well down to shield my face. I walked with my head bent, and before I reached the smithy, from whence no smoke rose this day, I cut through the back of someone else's property and so came to the shed that stood behind the Goodmans' house.

All the way, throughout that long and fitful journey, I'd been able to feel Mallie calling me, her desire bright in my mind. My heart beat because she needed me; I wanted to reassure her more than I wanted to breathe, yet once having arrived, I did not know how.

If she lay ill, as I feared, she could not arise and come to me, no matter how I called back to her. There would be people inside. I could not, in this case, knock at the door.

As I stood there, just within the doorway of the shed, the doctor's cart drove up. He alit and hurried in.

Another agony of waiting ensued. I do not know how long I hid there, my desperation rising, along with my anger.

I loved her, loved her as no one else did or ever would. I should have the right to go to her when she needed me, despite who or what I might be.

I could hear nothing from inside the house, a dwelling far grander than Sir's lowly cottage. I could hear only the wind wailing 'round the shed, the sleet hissing down outside, the pounding of my own heart—

and Mallie calling to me.

Even as I stood there, her calls grew weaker.

What would she think if she kept calling and I failed to come? What would she feel? The answer to that question at last drew me from the shed to the back of the house. I peered in through the nearest window, wishing myself invisible.

I saw a kitchen with a big stone sink, table, hearth. Several women occupied the space, Mallie's sisters and a woman I knew to be her mother, who sat with her face in her hands, weeping.

My heart nearly dropped through my boots, seeing that. I abandoned that window for the next and the next, abandoning also my caution and calling to Mallie in my mind, *I am here, love. I am here!*

The third window showed me a small room that had three beds in it, only one of them occupied. The doctor leaned over that bed, and the smith—Mr. Goodman—stood in the doorway. Neither of them noticed me.

Mallie! She lay in the bed, her hair a tousle of light brown curls. I could not see her face, but as I watched she tried to turn toward the window.

To me.

Mallie, love!

I had a sudden flashback to Ma, lying on the cot by the fire, overwhelmed by a fever of the lungs. Aye, but Mallie was young and strong.

And she'd come to harm by crossing the downs to see me, just as Ma had come to harm out in the weather doing chores I should have done.

My fault, my fault, my fault.

The refrain set up such a clamor I could barely hear

Mallie call to me again. But inside, the doctor arose and gestured to Mr. Goodman. They both stepped out of the room.

I knew I had only moments. My hands began forcing the window almost before the door closed behind them. Sealed by ice, it refused to open.

I used magic. I pulled it up from the roots of the earth, the first time I'd ever done so with such determination. I didn't even think about it, but the ice melted, and the sash swung in.

I was at her side in a trice, hunkered beside the bed with my hands on her, hood shrugged back so she could see me.

"I'm here, Mallie. Here."

"Rum Paul."

Oh, what did I see when I looked into her face? Flushed and feverish, her lips looked chapped, and her eyes burned with an other-worldly light. Her fingers, clasped in mine, felt scorching hot.

"I came," I murmured to her in fear and grief. "I came. You must get better, aye? Because I need you. You have no idea how much."

"I love you, Rum Paul. I wanted you to come so I could tell you that. I will love you always. You will remember me?"

"Blessed girl, you'll be with me. I'll fight for it, hear? I'll get rights to the cottage, and I'll make us a living. I'll change who I am—"

She said faintly, "Don't you dare. Don't ever change who you are."

"Mallie—"

"List to me, Rum Paul. I have little time." She seized my fingers and gazed into my eyes. "I will return to you. I cannot say when or in what guise—woman or child—but I promise I will return. Will you know me when I do?"

My throat closed. I had to force out the single word. "Aye." I would know her in any guise, or so I believed then.

I kissed her on the forehead and both cheeks, burning my lips. "I will wait for you. But, Mallie, you have to get well."

She disregarded that. "I do not want to die here."

"You won't die, darling girl."

"I want to die out on the downs, where I've been happy with you."

"You ain't dying."

"Please, Rum Paul."

An impossibility. But I rose with her in my arms and turned to the window. I'd thrown one leg over the sill and was half the way out when the door of the room opened.

Mallie's father stood there with her mother behind him.

He took in the scene, and his eyes bulged. He bellowed, "Thief! Thief!" and rushed into the room.

Chapter Ten

I fought them for all I was worth. I fought when they hauled me—us—back over the sill, and fought like a wild beast when they wrested Mallie from my arms. But there were too many of them—Mr. Goodman, swiftly followed by the hulking George and another of Mallie's brothers, and lastly by the fellow I knew to be Jules Longford.

I kicked, punched, and bit. I called up the magic again and slammed them with it over and over. But they struck me also, hit me in the head so many times my senses swam, and they at last overwhelmed me, bearing me to the floor.

All the while, they called me terrible names—elf and boggart and troll—all things I was not. And all the while I could hear Mallie wailing piteously in a weak voice that did not even sound like hers.

When at last they dragged me back up, I got a glimpse of the room. Mallie's mother and sister held her captive on the bed. The four men stood around me, Longford with me in his clutches, the others facing me in a half circle.

"Who are you? Why were you trying to take my daughter?" Goodman bellowed.

I said nothing but looked at Mallie. Blood trickled down my cheek and every one of my instincts howled: *trapped, trapped.*

George answered, "He's that unnatural creature belongs to the Stillskins. What d'you want with my sister?"

"A faery?" Goodman backed off a step, but Longford's hard grip on me did not waver.

"Look at him!" George cried. "Just look."

My hood had fallen back onto my shoulders during the struggle. Brutally, George tugged at my hair to reveal my ears. "Look at those. And them eyes. He sure as hell ain't human."

As a man, they made the sign against evil, all except Longford, whose hands were occupied.

Mallie spoke from the bed. "Leave him alone. I love him."

The men turned on her. "Daughter, if you think you do, 'tis because he's magicked you. Probably made you fall ill, too. Can't you see what this thing is?"

Thing.

My eyes met Mallie's across the room. She looked terrible, weak and waxen. Her eyes burned.

Barely audible now, she murmured, "I love him."

Goodman looked at George. "We'll prove it to her. Go get a bar from the forge."

I trembled in Longford's grip. I didn't know what they meant, not then, but it wouldn't be good. I had visions of them ramming a bar down—or up—me.

It would have been better if they had.

Goodman told Longford and his other son, "Bare him."

One of the women moaned. I struggled once more, to no avail. They tore off my coat and the ragged shirt beneath, but stopped there. George returned with a stout length of iron in his hands.

Goodman told Mallie, "I don't know exactly what this thing is, Daughter, but he's from the faerie realm, and he's been deceiving you. I'll prove it. Did you know faeries can't tolerate the touch of iron?"

I had only a vague idea of it. Being close to iron, or touching it, made me feel ill. I was well aware I hated tools—I'd thought that just meant I opposed the idea of work. Most tools and implements, though, had wooden handles, so I rarely touched iron itself.

If I did, I felt mildly queasy. So nothing prepared me for what was to come next.

"Hold him," Goodman ordered.

Longford hauled me up in front of him. Goodman took the stout iron bar from George. Raising it in his hands, he thrust it lengthwise flat against the bare skin of my chest.

Pain exploded all across my body, everywhere the iron touched. Never had I known—or imagined—such pain. Not when Sir hit or kicked me. Not when the village boys—George among them—stoned me. This burned with cold like the touch of a thousand icicles. It paralyzed me. It stole any notion of magic.

I screamed. I threw back my head and shrieked. Mallie's scream mingled with mine.

They drew the bar away then, but only to lay it on again in another place, up on my shoulder and kissing my cheek. My legs gave way beneath me; only Longford's fierce grip kept me from falling.

"See, Daughter," Goodman cried, "see what this creature is! Fey and unnatural."

Fully paralyzed now, I could only gasp hoarsely, my brain afire with pain, and watch as Mallie rose up, reaching for me before collapsing in her mother's arms.

She moved no more.

Now, you tell me—did I kill her, or did they?

I do not remember much after that. Just the pain, the weakness, and my desperation for Mallie. For even at that moment, my fear for her was greater than my fear for myself.

Her mother wailed. The men pulled the bar away, and George punched me, a blow I barely felt at the time. They all rushed to the bed.

I will return to you. I promise. Will you know me?

I will know you, always.

****

"What should we do with it?"

"Is it still alive?"

"Breathing, curse it."

Voices, above me, came to my ears like waves against the shore. I figured I should know them, but all my senses had been seared to dust. Somewhere deep in my mind, her name echoed over and over again. *Mallie, Mallie.* But not much else felt real. I'm not sure I even knew I remained in danger, or that it mattered then.

"Throw it outside."

"To come back again like a damned stray cat?"

"The cold will finish it."

"They're hard to kill."

Another voice, rough with grief. "It killed Mallie."

Mallie dead. The remaining shreds of my life, held together by mere whispers of hope, fell apart. I cared not what they did to me.

"Finish it off."

"Pa, that's murder. Even of a—a faerie."

"I don't care. Put the knife in it."

What followed outshone all the rest of it for agony.

One of them—George, I think—thrust a knife in me, deep into my side—a dire enough deed, given the blade contained iron. The pain in my flesh rose past enduring and everything went dark.

I awoke an immeasurable length of time later, out on the downs. 'Twas the pain that roused me, traveling along the courses of my veins, like liquid fire. They'd not bothered to replace my shirt or coat; I lay half on my side and half on my face, near frozen. A pool of my own blood had collected under me, and the handle of the knife still protruded from my side.

I groaned and rolled over, flopping onto my back helpless as a gaffed fish, and stared at the sky. Sleet continued to fall; it struck me in the face like sharp needles.

I did not know what had kept me alive. The cold should have completed what the Goodmans started. Yet I lived. I did not want to, but I did.

Mallie.

Had I imagined it all? Was she truly dead?

If so, it was them who had killed her, not me.

The truth of that made me gasp and started up the pain again. I wanted to hurt them as they'd wounded me—mortally.

To do so, I needed to live. Besides which… Besides which there was something, a single reason to live: Mallie had promised she'd come back to me.

I didn't believe in much, heaven knew, but I believed that. I believed Mallie's promises.

I had to live, and I had to wait.

I'm not sure how long it took me to stir from my place on the ground, or from whence the strength came. From anger, perhaps, or longing. At last I sat up, my head spinning in slow circles, and looked at the handle of the knife still protruding from my left side. The pain of the blade within my flesh screamed along every pathway, making it nearly impossible to think; it must have missed any nearby organ by a mere hair.

It needed to come out.

I had little strength left at that moment, but I gripped the hilt with both hands and bared my teeth in a snarl. I thought of the Goodmans and how much I hated them. I pulled.

The iron hurt as much coming out as going in. I must have blacked out again for a time. When I regained my senses, I could feel time had passed; night edged into morning. I didn't know where I was.

Help me, Mallie.

But I had no strength left for magic, and my connection to her had snapped the instant she collapsed in her mother's arms.

I'll return to you.

I dragged myself home to the shepherd's hut. I didn't know where I was, not consciously, but some inner instinct took me there, that which knew every foot of the downs. I don't remember crawling into the hut, or into the pile of blankets that served me as a bed, but I must have, for I awakened there some few days later and, weak as a newborn, took stock of myself.

The deep cut in my side had closed, leaving a ridged scar. Well, I'd always been a quick healer, so I didn't find that too surprising.

The iron bar, however, had left livid marks where they'd laid it against my skin. Across my chest, in red, I bore its outline, as well as on my shoulder and cheek. Reminders I did not need.

Like any animal in its den, I laid up in the hut. I did not want the Goodmans or Longford to know I'd survived.

I was not sure I had survived, not all of me, anyway. The better part of me, that which had lived for Mallie, had surely died there with her, in that terrible room.

Chapter Eleven

Eventually when strength afforded, I went down to the churchyard and looked at her grave. I had to do that, I think, to prove to myself she truly was dead, though I knew it, in my heart, because she no longer lingered, like the whisper of a song, in my mind. Memory kept her there, aye—while healing, I relived our moments together a thousand times. They lent me comfort and torment in equal measures. I longed for the touch of her hand, and I think I needed to see, with my own eyes, proof she had left the world.

But I had to be careful venturing to the village, and it took a long while for sufficient strength to return. My body healed; my spirit did not.

How did I survive the rest of that winter? I'm sure I do not know. I stole food; I stole clothing. I ate things that should have killed me but did not. Part of me, perhaps the better part, wanted very badly to die.

I turned into someone I did not know. Not the boy—faerie or otherwise—that Mallie had loved and who'd loved her. I became instead a bitter wretch who no longer sang and who thought far too often of revenge.

Revenge makes a poisoned diet, the absence of love a bitter draught.

In an effort to cover the scar on my cheek, I grew out my beard. I no longer stood straight but hunched with pain. One night, I crept down and set fire to the shed at the back of Goodman's property. Then I hid and watched it burn.

I'd always loved fire, liked watching it and the pictures that danced in the flames. I didn't like what I saw in these, but I did find satisfaction in setting that building ablaze. The wind blew high that night, and sparks set the house afire, though the forge, out front, did not burn. Ironic, isn't it? Goodman worked every day with fire, and no doubt thought he'd tamed it, yet he couldn't stand against these flames.

He and his family came running out of the house like vermin. The women wailed; they all stood and watched their home burn.

I went away, after, with the flames still dancing in my eyes.

I began haunting the farm again, going there at night and peering in the windows at Sir. At times I performed acts of mischief—set all Ma's hens loose, spilled the grain in the bins, and once pulled Sir's cart way out onto the downs, where I left it. I disturbed his cache of rum bottles, for I knew where he kept those, and hid them from him. Sometimes I slept in the byre with the animals, who remembered me, and it felt warmer than the hut.

I began to think how fine it would be if the farm were mine.

Indeed, before the winter ended, I grew tired of the shepherd's hut. My only real aim in staying there had been for a place to meet with Mallie. Now, bereft of other comfort, I wanted that of Sir's fireside, and he— as I assured myself—deserved a comeuppance.

So I increased my campaign against him. I

misplaced the things he used every day, I stole his boots and put out the fire with a wee wish of magic for, aye, that had returned to me. I left the doors to the byre open, I hid his pipe, and whispered to him while he slept.

In truth, Sir slept seldom and little enough in his bed. More often did he doze by the fire with his rum and that pipe close at hand.

I thought again about starting a fire as I had at the Goodmans' and roasting him. But I saw how the tricks I played annoyed him, and that gave me satisfaction.

An impatient man always, he hated looking for things. I began hiding everything he touched or needed and then standing by in the room, disguised by magic, to watch the fun.

Once or twice, when he'd just awakened, I let him have a wee glimpse of me. At first I think he did not know me, changed by the beard. But once, staring into my eyes, he groaned, "Rum?"

"I got out, as you ordered me," I told him just before disappearing. "Now I'm back again."

My magic was a new kind—dark, powerful, and as bitter as I was. It came to me, on the wings of the hate that filled me, ever more easily.

I decided Sir should die of natural causes, spurred by fright. But it took a while, him being a tough old bugger.

Not so tough, though, as me.

Most of the winter passed before he became truly rattled. In the end, I took everything that mattered to him—his rum, his pipe and tobacco, his means of getting his product to the coast. I even disguised the still with glamour so he believed it lost.

When I felt ready—when I judged him ready—I let him see me standing beside him one evening, there by the fire.

He started like a man seeing a ghost. He'd had no rum, only a few swallows of his own rotgut. I marked the change in him—he looked older, thinner. And when he looked at me, I could see the fear.

"Rum? How in hell d'ye get in? I barred the door."

"Surely you know I don't need to use the door."

He looked at the windows, tight shut.

"Or those," I told him. "It's magic."

He began to swear in a stream. "You accursed, unnatural creature! I never should have let her bring you into this house. But she never had a child, and she wanted you."

"You should have strangled me, back then."

"So I should."

"Because now, I'm going to strangle you. And then I'm going to enjoy living in this cottage, and I'm going to reap the rewards of your business. As your son and heir."

"You ain't no son of mine."

"I know."

"You a damned boggart, or somewhat. Something from the dark side."

"I know. And I'm very hard to kill. But you're not."

I drew up a stool and sat opposite the bench where he'd always sat—spent most his time all my life, in fact. Oh, he'd got up to run his liquor, shout at Ma, or thump me, but not often.

Conversationally, I told him, "Let's talk about evil. I suppose you think I am that."

He tried to chuckle and failed dismally. Fear now had him by the throat. He'd never been afraid of me in the past, and I found this a heady experience.

"You're the very personification of evil, boy."

"I think that you are. The way you treated Ma, the way you treated me."

"How should I treat a damned faerie? I let her keep you, didn't I? You should thank me. I might have sent you to church, where the roof would have fallen on your head."

"As it would on you. In some ways we are two of a kind, you and me. It comes down to who is stronger. Which of us will win?"

"Get out o' my house, vile creature."

"No, I've decided I'm staying. What will you do about it?"

I could see him contemplate that, and wonder what he could do. Did he have the strength to toss me out?

He stirred on the bench and attempted to rise. I held him down magically, with a wish. Realizing I had power over him, he began to sweat.

I smiled. "Now we wait."

His eyes widened so I could see white all around the dull blue. He cursed and struggled. He called me every manner of name he could devise, some I'd never heard before. His strength began to fade, and I waited, hands loosely linked, holding the wish in my mind with all my ability and staring, staring at him.

"This is a comfortable enough cottage," I told him at length. "Not grand. Not good enough for Mallie, probably, but plenty good enough for me. 'Twill be better still with your stink gone out of it."

He tried to speak, tried to make some reply, but

fear had him so full by the throat now he could do naught more than groan.

"I'll continue to run the business. Joe knows me." I grinned at him. "Don't worry, I'll be all right."

He writhed, trying to escape the bench, his arms twisting and his face a rictus of desperation.

I got up. I wasn't tall, it's true. I was scarred. I was, as had been borne upon me, *other*. But I felt the full of my power then, dark and deep.

How had I failed to realize Mallie kept me from the darkness?

I bent over the old man and stared full into his face. "For all the times you were cruel to me and to Ma and to them animals out there, I want you to know I'm paying you back." And I bared my teeth at him. "Die."

Was it a wish? A suggestion? A command? I only knew he obeyed it. For once in his long and nasty life, he did what somebody else wanted.

I never touched him. I touched nothing. Afterward I went away like I'd never been there. I returned to the shepherd's hut and stayed for what felt like months but couldn't have been more than a week.

Then I went back to the cottage. Sir's corpse was gone. The place looked tidy, the way it hadn't since Ma's passing. Someone had been feeding the animals— a neighbor, most likely—though no one was there.

I settled in, built a fire, and slept that night in my old bed in the loft. I couldn't bear entering Ma's room, not then.

The next day I walked to the nearest neighbor, Mr. Newcomb, and asked about the animals. He admitted he'd been looking after them.

"So you're back, are you?" he asked.

"Aye. Thank you kindly, but I won't need your help anymore. Farm's mine now."

He never argued it. Nobody did. Who would want so poor a place as Sir had let it become, tucked in at the edge of the downs?

No one came. I lived alone and saw only Joe, who seemed relieved when I turned up.

"Ah, lad, I heard about your old man's passing, and wondered what would happen to the business."

"I mean to keep on with it."

"All right."

"Just one change," I told him. "I don't need that rum no more. I'll have coin instead."

He didn't look pleased. Neither did he refuse. Henceforth, he paid me in coin for the loads I dragged to the cave. Winter became spring, a spring without Mallie. Her family must have heard what had become of me, that I hadn't died when they left me out on the downs. I do not know what they thought, but I do suspect they spread rumors of me.

About what I was—some sort of dark faerie.

About what I wasn't—human.

Folk whispered behind my back and almost always made the sign against evil when they encountered me. Sometimes boys came out from the town and threw stones or eggs at my cottage. A show of my face or a wee wish would chase them off again.

I kept to myself and left the Goodmans, for their sins, strictly alone. And I waited for Mallie's promise to come true.

Part Two

Laura Strickland

Chapter Twelve

Time passed, a great deal of time. I changed, although I barely aged. In youth, I'd grown quickly and stopped early. Now, the process seemed to slow within me. Years went by, then decades, and still I waited.

I changed inwardly more than physically; with Mallie's passing, something inside me had died, most likely the small measure of innocence I'd possessed. I lost the impish love for mischief that had been so much a part of me, the involuntary response to beauty. The only songs I sang were rattling ditties tied to my magic.

For the magic endured within me, but like my spirit it became dark and secretive. Powerful, it could flow from me without effort when I chose—when I wished. Because wishing still made the conduit through which I could make desires turn true.

All but one.

After a while, when I peered into the cracked mirror that hung on the wall of the cottage, I no longer recognized myself. A black beard obscured the lower half of my face. I wore a cap pulled well down over my black hair, now most often shorn, and rarely could I meet the expression in my own green eyes.

I worried that when Mallie returned—and I clung to the belief she would—she'd fail to know me. *Promise you will know me*, she'd begged, but she'd made no such promise in return, and it seemed plain she'd never equate the small, wizened man—so obviously part fae—with the lithe boy she'd known.

But my heart…my heart loved her still.

For a long time, I haunted the places we'd shared together. I visited the shepherd's hut and each hollow where we'd lingered to sing songs. I hiked, in turn, to the kistvaens, menhirs, and other standing stones. Part of me thought I'd find her there waiting for me.

Sometimes I thought I saw her, putting flowers on her own grave or walking toward me along the road. For a long time, I thought I saw her ghost. Now I think those I saw must have been members of her family, descendants.

For, aye, that much time passed. Generations. Joe aged and perished and was replaced by his grandson, with whom I continued to do business. Mallie's parents died of old age; George married, raised a family, and aged in turn, his hair turning silver.

As Mallie's would have?

The village changed. It grew. A new road went through, giving it a crossroads. Soldiers came—invaders—and a castle was built on the rise just to the north. A man set himself up there as king.

Many of the Goodmans' descendants turned to farming. They supported the new king and, for all I knew, lived happily enough beneath him. I survived on the fringes, Sir's farm mostly overgrown, no crops and no animals. Folk forgot I existed.

A century passed, two; the only things that remained the same were the downs and the fervent wishes in my heart.

****

The first time I saw her was on a bright, windy day,

round about April, I expect, though I no longer kept strict track of the seasons. Truth be told, I kept track of little—sometimes it felt I existed in a cocoon and little of the world reached me.

But seeing her jolted me from my stupor, right enough.

On my way to fulfill a wish, I walked along the lane below the castle with a sack over my shoulder. For, aye, I still fulfilled wishes, but only when they pulled at me strongly enough. When they were fervent, I could hear them. They came to me on the wind like echoes of songs I had sung long ago, and then, for her sake, I could not resist.

When I fulfilled such wishes, I did so always for Mallie, in hopes of creating beauty for her as once I had. Aye, well, it didn't make sense, not even to me.

This particular afternoon I made my way to the far side of the village with a kitten in the sack. The kitten had black-and-white-patched fur and an orange spot on its left ear. A little girl had spent weeks longing for it, until I could no longer bear to listen.

She'd lost her own cat—that looked just like this one—to an accident. I knew how it felt to lose what was loved and to long for it back.

That very thought hovered in my mind that afternoon when I looked up and saw Mallie walking toward me along the lane.

You cannot imagine how I felt. Or perhaps, having heard my story so far, you can. Everything within me froze, and there, with the sack across my shoulder, I stumbled to a halt.

She had golden-brown hair like Mallie's, all blown by the breeze into disarray around a face that blushed like a rose. Wide blue eyes regarded me with curiosity from beneath feathered brows. She moved with the light, easy grace I remembered and smiled at me as she came along, humming a tune.

One of my tunes.

My heart, which had known so much sorrow, faltered within me before it began to beat double time. The thing I had wished for so long, while I made all wishes besides my own come true, stared me in the face.

She had come, she had come back to me.

"Good afternoon, sir," she bade me as she passed, and a dimple clove her cheek. I knew that dimple, had kissed it, had sought to encourage it with my nonsense.

The powers help me, I made no reply to the lass's bright greeting. But I turned in the path when she passed, and watched her go.

Did she know me, as I knew her? Nay, I think not, even though she hummed my tune.

How did she know the song I had made up from the joy of a day on the downs, and a windy sky?

And who was she? Who, in this life? For Mallie, my Mallie, had rested two centuries in her grave. How could I find her again in a village full of strangers?

I delivered the kitten and went home to contemplate the miracle. The wishing that poured from me after that must have been prodigious, indeed. I could feel it bubbling, dark, dark but shot through with such brightness it fair frightened me.

Love, as I had learned, opened a man up to sorrow. But seeing her had lit hope inside me, and it refused to fade.

I haunted the village after that, determined to see

her again. I could render myself all but invisible when I chose, and I took to frequenting the places such a young woman might go. The shops, the market, the flower stalls beneath the castle. I got nary a glimpse of her in return.

But she existed. I knew that now.

I needed to see her again the way I used to need seeing Mallie, out on the downs, in the days when our bright desire would call to one another.

I believe that desire called her to me again, for I was not without means.

An event was announced, a celebration of May Day. A festival was planned, and a ribband pole was erected on the castle grounds. Everywhere I went in the village, I heard folk speak of little else. The king, whose name was Alfred, had invited the daughters of landowners from all the country round, with the object of choosing a wife to replace his that had died.

Why he needed a festival to make such a choice, I never could tell. But so the tale went.

The entire village, it seemed, took part in preparing for the festival. Like many others, and with my broad-brimmed hat pulled well down over my face, I went to watch.

The village lasses busied themselves decorating the May pole with flowers, along with the raised platform that fronted it.

She was there. I saw her almost at once, for she shone among the other young women like a jewel among gray stones. She wore a dress of dusty rose that day, which picked up the color of her cheeks, and a white apron. She had her hair arranged just the way Mallie used to, part of it gathered atop her head and the rest tumbling down her back. Looking at her, I could smell Mallie's hair again, the fragrance of it when I would press my face against her neck, even after so many years.

I tell you, it gave me a new lease on life, it did. I felt almost like the lad I had been, as if I wanted to dance and sing along with those lasses.

I stood and watched till they finished their tasks. Then, half hidden, I followed her home. She went in company with another, younger girl—blonde, like her. Curiously, they passed right by the blacksmith's shop, now run by one of George's descendants, and they waved to its occupants.

Goodmans, then? Was she still a Goodman?

I followed them a long way, to a farm out past the village, halfway to Underhill. A prosperous enough place, it looked well kept. The two girls went in through the gate, and I lost sight of her.

I needed to know her name. I needed to speak with her. I went home and built a fire in the hearth.

My affinity for fire had remained with me. Both fascinated and beguiled by it, I could still often see pictures of what had happened and what was to come. I'd seen Mallie's death over again, many times, and as a result I used the ability sparingly.

But I looked, now.

I saw her dressed in fine clothes. I saw her with a babe in her arms, rocking it. Was it my child? But she did not look happy.

A song came into my head.
What's in a name?
If you know mine
And guess in time

It's all the same.
Give me your child
She shall be wild.
She it is who's mine.

I wanted to dance to that song. At the same time, for some reason, it made me shudder.

I did not want the babe; I merely wanted Mallie back again.

Chapter Thirteen

Luck, good or bad, does not exist. There's merely wishing. Wish hard enough for something and it will come to you. Focus hard enough on something and that will come to you also, even if it's something you do not want. It's all about the calling.

I'd been calling Mallie back to me for over two centuries. The downs are old, and I don't expect two centuries meant a lot to them. They aged slowly, even more slowly than me.

Beneath my whiskers and burn scars, down at the bones, I remained a young man. The magic that made up the bones of the downs didn't age either. The trick came in using it properly.

My longing urged me to act, but my head preached for caution. I wanted to go to that farm, knock on the door, and ask for her. After all, she was mine. But I knew how I appeared to others, and I'd waited too long to spoil my chances now.

I had to get near her, and I had to make it count.

One thing hadn't changed; men in small boats still ran smuggled goods all up and down the coast. My contact there, named Jeb, made one of my few sources of information, so I went and met with him.

Jeb, a canny man in his late thirties, and the latest in a whole line of Joe's successors, always treated me with a measure of respect. He had no idea who Sir had been; nor had he dealt with me long enough to tell I didn't age. He called me Mr. Stills, the balance of my name having been lost over the years, so that no one knew it. In fact, Jeb once had quipped that my name matched my illegal profession.

On this occasion, as we loaded the swill into his boat and unloaded the empty kegs for next time, he did me the favor of introducing the very subject I wanted to discuss.

"Lots o' excitement up your way, so I hear, Mr. Stills."

I paused in my work to eye him from beneath the brim of my hat. "The festival, aye," I returned. "Will ye be there?"

"My wife wouldn't miss it."

First indication I'd had that Jeb had a wife. He went on, "Not every day a king throws a party for the whole district."

"Aye," I drawled. "He's never before been so generous." I knew little enough about Alfred, just that his forefather had battled his way into the country, built that castle, and moved in, declaring the area his.

Fool—the downs were, quite certainly, mine.

Jeb snorted. "He wants something, don't he? His kind usually do."

"A wife," I asserted.

"A new wife. Did you not hear? He lost the last one some year or more ago. Died in childbed, she did, trying to give him a son. Child died too."

I'd never met King Alfred, had only rarely set eyes on the man, but that caused me a twinge of feeling for him. We might have little in common, him being a man of wealth and stature, and I a man of the downs. But I knew how it felt to lose the woman I loved.

"A hard road," I murmured.

"Ain't it? Don't rightly know where I'd be if I lost my Meg."

"Broken."

"Broken, aye, Mr. Stills. Yet Alfred's a king and must get an heir. 'Tis said he wants a bride with extraordinary abilities."

"What's that mean?"

Jeb leaned his head toward me and lowered his voice. "Magic."

A shock went through me, and I tried to scoff. "Does that still exist?"

"Well, sure it do, Mr. Stills. There's magic in the fog that comes and hides our boats when we're running the coast, and in the dark that covers our wake."

"And on the downs."

He nodded vigorously. "There, most of all."

"Tell me, Jeb, what do you know about a family called Goodman?"

Caution came into his eyes, but he only said, "Lots of Goodmans here about. That's an old family."

"Aye. These have a farm off toward Little Underhill, with a big white house."

"Ah, George Goodman." The name made me start, though Jeb went right on talking. A different George Goodman, plainly. "He's a canny man with a lot o' ambition, so he is. Why do you ask, Mr. Stills?"

"I've been hearing about him, that's all. Has a big family, does he?"

"Three daughters, I believe, and three sons. The eldest daughter's a beauty."

"Is she?" I asked innocently, though my heart

skipped a beat.

"Aye, goes by the name of Maisie. George never stops bragging on her, but then he's a bragging sort of fellow."

"I see." That bit of news gave me a sick feeling in the pit of my stomach. "Well, thank you, Jeb, for the news."

"Sure thing, Mr. Stills." He placed a stack of coins on my palm. "Will I see you at the festival?"

"I doubt that, Jeb. I very much doubt you'll see me."

****

Following that conversation, I went home and made my plans. I built up a fire and consulted it. I saw her there, Maisie—the name wasn't really so different, was it, from Mallie?

I believed it, then, believed that after so long she'd returned to me.

With the help of things seen in the fire, I hatched a plan. I went out, got my cart, and hauled it to Little Underhill, a not inconsiderable feat, though it failed to tire me over much. Once there, I used all the coin Jeb had paid me on a variety of purchases.

Returned home, I made further preparations. I stripped down, washed myself, and donned some of the clothing I'd bought. Ordering myself to calm, I summoned up a small spell of glamour, just enough to alter my appearance, and set out.

When I entered the village, I began with my cry, "Tinker! Tinker!" Others like me already circulated the place, peddlers of everything from sweets to bright banners. I sold a few things but made sure to keep the best items hidden.

I reached Goodman's farm just past noon and paused long enough to rearrange the goods for sale. I'd decorated the ancient cart with ribbons and flowers, and I paused at the farm gate with my cry of "Tinker!"

They came running, all of Goodman's daughters and a couple of housemaids, too, in a gaggle that surrounded the cart. She came at the head of them, her hair gleaming in the warm sun, her eyes bright with interest.

"Oh, girls," she cried, "a tinker. How lucky is this?"

There's no such thing as luck.

She paused beside me with her hands on the cart, so near I might have touched her. I stared in amazement. She was Mallie, or the spit of her—rose-petal skin, slender form, and sweet, high breasts. Her wide blue eyes regarded me with well-remembered curiosity.

"Have I seen you before, Master Peddler?"

"Aye."

"I thought I knew all the tradesmen here about. But I don't remember you."

The other girls paid no attention to me but pawed through the goods in the cart, coming up with ribbons and beads and the like—all I'd set there to lure them.

Maisie's two sisters, nearly as pretty as she, twittered like birds. One of the housemaids looked older, the second of an age with the sisters, a wee thing with brown hair.

I leaned toward Maisie, near enough so I could catch her sweet scent, and whispered, "Miss, I have the perfect trinket for you."

"Have you?" she returned, smiling at me in delight.

Just so would Mallie look at me when I revealed I'd made her a new song. *Sing it for me*.

"Aye." My heart leaped within my chest and then settled into a contented rhythm. She had come; she'd come back to me.

"Show me."

"Here." Not in the cart after all, I drew it from my pocket and held it out on the palm of my hand. "Special, this is."

"Oh!" Her lips parted like rose petals preparing to fall. "It's magic, is that. I can tell."

So she could still recognize magic, could she?

"Aye. Here, hold it in your hand."

The bauble, a pendant with a tiny rose quartz stone, slid from my palm to hers.

She lifted her eyes to my face in amazement. "It tingles! I can feel the magic."

"Aye. You're a clever girl, you are. Not everyone can sense that."

"I've always believed in magic."

So she would. "You wear that to the festival," I told her, "and you'll be the most beautiful lass there." She already was the most beautiful lass anywhere.

"Aye."

The small brown maid came up to us. "Miss Maisie, what's that?"

Maisie ignored her. "How much do you want for it?" she asked me.

"But a penny."

"It must be worth far more."

"It is," the maid put in. She sent me such a searching look that, for the briefest moment, I feared she could see through the thin veneer of glamour.

"There must be some treachery in it."

"Jenny, you'll not tell me what to do."

"Never. I would not think to try," Jenny averred.

Maisie plucked the ribbon from her palm and held up the pendant. "It's magic, see?"

"That's what I'm afraid of."

Maisie lowered her voice. "You know Pa wants me to catch the king's eye."

"Don't know why he'd want you to do that," the brown maid sniffed.

Nor did I, and I didn't like the way it made me feel. I didn't like that at all.

Chapter Fourteen

Had the fire betrayed me? Or had my own intention led me wrong? Either way, for better or worse, the pendant rested in Maisie's hand.

She paid me her penny. In truth, pennies showered me, but I tucked the one she placed in my palm into the hem of my shirt, close against my skin.

Pulling the cart home again, selling the last of my goods along the way, I reflected that perhaps the fire hadn't failed me after all. I'd gone to Goodman's farm to meet but one person, and in that I had succeeded.

Before leaving, I'd leaned close to Maisie and said, "Be sure and wear that, now, to the fair."

"I'll wear it always."

"And if you need me, clasp that stone in your hand and wish. I'll come."

She hadn't asked why she might need me, a peddler. She'd gazed into my eyes and nodded.

I left, sure she'd remember.

That night, I slept better than I had in a century. She'd returned to me, Mallic had. She wore the stone, and we had a connection. She might well catch the king's eye at the start of the festivities, next day. But no king would wed the daughter of a simple farmer. He would choose one of the guests he'd invited from afar. And Mallie would be mine.

Only two things did I fail to understand: my dream

of her holding a babe, and why the thought of her and the king together kept flitting through my mind.

I should have seen the danger in these things, I who understood the nature of wishing. But I felt half mad with the joy of her return and lost the better part of my caution.

The festivities at the castle began early that next day. There were jugglers and vendors selling food, and musicians set up playing tunes. I went in the same disguise as that I'd worn yesterday—that of an older man—anxious to get a glimpse of Maisie.

One of the first people I saw was the king.

Funny how, up to now, he'd barely impacted my life, and him a man of such importance. But tucked away in my cottage at the edge of the downs, I usually escaped notice. I had never exchanged so much as a look with him.

Now, though, he came down from the castle with an entourage of guests and servants. Several in that train were women—candidates, I could only suppose, to fill the place of his wife who had died trying to give him a son. Beholding him, I could understand his haste to remarry, for he was no longer young, though not elderly either, by any means. Such men—men of importance—must see to their futures.

I fancied I could tell a great deal about him just by looking. Probably in his late thirties, he had brown hair and a haughty, handsome face. He wore a fine crimson robe trimmed with spotted fur, and sported a narrow golden crown on his head, as if he wanted everyone who encountered him to know him for king.

Aye, I told myself, but I did not need to deal with the man. For me, he represented but a means to an end.

A pavilion had been set up opposite the May pole, and after touring the grounds, Alfred settled there in fine state, with his companions all around him.

A crowd gathered to watch the jugglers. Alfred watched them, too, and sent out a troop from his following who proved to be acrobats and also performed. All in all, the activities evinced a happy and excited mood.

Folk kept arriving from all 'round; eventually a large group came from Goodman's farm. The sisters and maids from yesterday were there, along with a group of young men so like the George Goodman of my time they could only be Maisie's brothers.

Ah, such a cruel twist of fate that my Maisie should come back to me tainted by Goodman blood.

No matter; I saw little but Maisie. She wore blue, a heavenly color for her, and had a wreath of flowers on her hair. She and the other girls giggled and blushed when young men in the crowd noticed them, and many did notice.

She'd come with what must be her parents, a matronly woman and a man who might have been an older version of the George Goodman I knew. He soon joined a group of other men near his age, who stood not far from the pavilion talking and drinking ale bought from the roving vendors.

Me, I could not take my eyes from Maisie. Wherever she went, I followed. She and the other lasses chattered like robins and flitted like sparrows. Men's eyes turned to them again and again.

I did not think anyone noticed me, disguised by my glamour, for I appeared nothing more than a wizened old man. Yet somehow I caught the notice of the little brown maid, Jenny. She glanced at me repeatedly, eventually pointing me out to Maisie and dragging her over to me by the arm.

"Why are you following us?" Jenny challenged, sticking out her little chin.

"Eh?" I returned. Her eyes, brown and speckled like a trout, regarded me so fiercely I momentarily forgot Maisie.

"It's the peddler from yesterday," that young woman exclaimed in apparent delight, reclaiming my attention. "Look, sir, I'm wearing your bauble."

She drew the little stone, dangling from its ribbon, from between her breasts. Her blue eyes sparkled at me joyously. "Now all my wishes will come true."

The maid rolled her eyes and said acerbically, "Why you think you'll gain the affections of the king, I cannot say."

"Not I, but Father thinks it." Again, Maisie looked at me. "Can you make it happen?" She pulled at the ribbon. "Can this?"

"Do not be foolish," Jenny told her. She switched her gaze back to me. "And stop following us."

"As you will, miss," I murmured, and tugged on the brim of my hat. The maid might not believe in my magic; Maisie did. That alone mattered.

The king once again left the pavilion to circulate among the ever-increasing crowd of villagers. The girls had rejoined their group, and I, holding hard to a spell of invisibility, remained close by. Thus I witnessed the moment he caught sight of Maisie and paused like a man arrested.

Who could blame him? Her beauty shone like a patch of blue sky on a rainy day. Even among the other girls she stood out, and visibly impacted him.

"Who is that?" I heard him ask one of the men who accompanied him, whom I took for an advisor but who, I later learned, held the post of castle bailiff. "The lass in blue."

"Permit me, sire, to make inquiries and find out."

The bailiff hurried off. Not long after, I saw him speaking at length with Maisie's father. All the while, the king stood watching Maisie, as reluctant as I to look away from her beauty.

And Maisie was well aware of his regard. Like any young woman, she played to it: she simpered; she sent gleaming looks in his direction; she tossed her golden head and smiled.

Misgiving once more stirred in my heart. I did not want her to desire the king, or anyone besides me. Yet she didn't remember all we'd shared or what she meant to me. What I meant to her.

I made sure to stand close by when the bailiff reported back to Alfred, strengthening my invisibility so they didn't know I was there. I heard their conversation.

"Well, Neil, who is she?"

"No one of importance, sire. Just the daughter of a farmer, and a boastful farmer to boot. He claims his daughter Maisie is a treasure beyond compare—untouched, matchless in all the area 'round, and gifted with magic."

"Maisie." The king repeated her name dreamily. And then, with a new note in his voice, "Magic?"

"So the fellow claims. He insists she was visited by a faerie soon after birth, and so blessed."

"Ah."

"It is, of course, nonsense."

"So you may say, Neil, but magic plays a part in many things."

"The farmer—Goodman—claims they are of good family and go way back in these parts, to the very first settlers. He implies the girl is worthy of your notice."

The king looked thoughtful. "He may not be far wrong."

"But, sire—"

"There's an ancient belief in these parts, Neil, about a king's connection to the land."

Aye, there was. Fancy this man believing in it, and in magic.

"I will speak with her father later. Before the start of the feast, bring him to me."

But she came back for me. She's supposed to be mine. Those words pounded through my mind, with the impact of the stones the village children used to throw.

I could not let the king—or anyone—come between us again. If she'd returned, it was for me.

Chapter Fifteen

"Who are you?"

The question turned my head, and I stared, startled, at the small lass who'd come up behind me. The brown maid, Jenny, stood only as high as my nose, but the fierce look in her eyes made up for her diminutive size.

Ah, and how had she seen through my glamour? I'd thought I stood well shaded by it, watching the festivities—watching Maisie enjoy the festivities. Yet Jenny had sniffed me out like a keen-nosed hound.

Before I could answer her query, she pressed, "You are certainly no ordinary peddler. And you are far too interested in Maisie."

"Every man here is interested in Miss Maisie."

She snorted and narrowed her clever brown eyes. "There is something odd about you," she asserted. "Something—otherwise."

I blinked at her. So she thought to know about me, did she? "We are all odd, in our ways," I informed her. "Anyway," I added, dropping just a bit of my glamour, "who are you to stand guard on your mistress?"

"She is more to me than just mistress. She is my friend, and I would not have you harm her in any way."

"Me, harm her?" I nodded toward the pavilion where the king still lounged among his many guests. "You should rather worry about how he might injure her."

"Aye? And how could the attentions of a king injure anyone?"

"You would be surprised."

A thoughtful look invaded her eyes. She reached out and grabbed my sleeve. "Come, we need to speak together, you and I."

Unprecedented, that—no one touched me, not voluntarily. True, her fingers clutched only the fabric of my sleeve, not my skin. Yet the shock of it caused me to follow along with her.

She led me to a sheltered place beside one of the hedgerows, where we sat side by side. It occurred to me she could prove useful, close to Maisie as she was, though I would first need to get her on my side.

But how? She could apparently see through my magic, and I possessed few other advantages.

The first thing she did now was untie a bundle and spread a small repast out on her knee. Shooting a look at me, she asked, "Do you want to share?"

"Is that your dinner?" I returned.

"Aye, I brought it from home. Unlike some, I have no pennies to waste on food or baubles."

"Thank you, Mistress Jenny, but no."

"You need not be afraid. 'Tis but brown bread and cheese, both of which I made myself."

"I am not afraid."

"Well then, I will eat while we talk, since naught has passed my lips since early this morning."

Considerably taken aback by her attitude, I said, "As you will, Mistress."

"You'd best call me Jenny. What is your interest in Maisie, Master Peddler? And pray, do not pretend it is not interest. I know better."

"Do you?" She threw me completely off balance, this small brown maid. Yet it would definitely benefit me to gain her favor. How much to tell her? How far could I trust her?

"You came to the farm the other day just to see her, didn't you?" she accused. "And to give her that bauble."

"Why would I do that?"

"Aye, Master Peddler, that very question has haunted me. I do not understand what you could want of her. You know little about her, other than what you see."

I went breathless. "Tell me about her, then."

"Why should I?"

"To redirect my interest, perhaps."

The small brown maid snorted. "She is rash and willful. She insists always on her own way. She does not always tell the truth."

Oh, if only I'd listened to the lass's words. Instead I spoke what was in my mind. "You are bent on warning me off."

"I am."

"Why?"

She shot me a quick look. "A good question. Cursed if I know. I have struggled all day long with the need to speak to you. As you can see, the impulse finally overwhelmed me."

"Aye," I murmured, still very much off balance.

"Master Peddler, she is not for you."

"Why?" I challenged yet again. "Because you think me poor and aged? Because—" I could hear the sharp note in my own voice "—you think I am not human?"

"So you are not," she agreed blithely, "at least not

wholly so. Part man and part faerie, possibly."

Again I stared. "You can't know…"

"I can't know, but I can sense it. And nay, that has naught to do with the matter at hand. I do not warn you off for Maisie's sake, but for your own."

I considered myself, by and large, to be perceptive. Perhaps, though, not so perceptive as she. Now I stared. "I do not understand."

She sighed. "Maisie may be a farmer's daughter, and I a maid, but she is also my closest friend. I was taken in as a foundling, see, by the Goodmans."

A foundling, just like me.

"We grew up together. So I know all her faults. And all her strengths."

I wondered, since they'd been raised together, why the Goodmans did not treat Jenny more as daughter than maid. Then I remembered Sir. She was not their daughter and never would be.

A bond between us, maybe. But I'd not waited two centuries for the small brown maid, despite how comfortable I felt in her company.

I said, "You just don't want me to spoil her chances with Alfred."

"Do you think you could?"

"Aye." I could help, or harm.

"And do you think she has a chance with a man of such high standing?"

"Aye," I said again.

"Ah, God! Fools upon fools. Let her go to the king if she will, Master Peddler. She is not meant for the likes of you."

There, for all her bright perceptiveness, was the brown maid wrong.

She popped the last of the cheese into her mouth and leaned her head close to mine. "And you may as well drop the magical disguise. You are no more an aged man than I."

****

The next day the festivities continued, and Maisie, with her father at her side, was invited to the castle. I hung about, continuing to mingle with those still reveling, and observed them when they reemerged some time later.

Maisie looked troubled and distracted. She hurried off immediately to join Jenny, who'd also remained nearby. The two of them went away together, speaking furiously.

But Farmer Goodman emerged looking pleased with himself and joined a group of his cronies standing by and drinking outside. I had no difficulty shifting close enough to hear, especially as he immediately started boasting in a loud voice.

"I told King Alfred, I did. I told him all about the Goodmans, what an old family we are hereabouts, old as the downs themselves, and here far longer than he's been in the district. That's what you need in a wife, I told him. A connection with the land. You want sons, that's the way to get them."

One of his cronies laughed. "I thought you got 'em by tossing the wife's skirts over her head."

The others joined in the laughter. They were all tipsy, including the verbose Goodman, who'd clearly imbibed while in the king's company.

But he sobered abruptly and flushed red with annoyance. "This is serious, Bert. My girl could become a queen. God knows, we're good enough—

better than him, when it comes to it." He tapped the side of his nose. "I just need something to tip the scales, see? To get them wed. After that—once our Maisie's his wife—it won't matter."

"What won't matter?" his friends pressed, but intoxicated as he was, he wouldn't say.

Me, I remembered the expression on Maisie's face, and dread flooded my heart. It was not ordinary dread, like I used to feel when I knew Sir, drunk and angry, waited to chastise me over some unfinished chore. This was deep and accompanied by the conviction that things were going in the wrong direction.

Impossible. I'd waited for Mallie to return to me, waited far too long; the fulfillment of her promise was at hand. And if I let myself think on things going wrong, they would. Therein lay the power of the magic. Yet panic, hard to subjugate, had its own power.

I told myself over and over again no king would marry the daughter of a humble farmer, however grand he believed himself.

But when I saw Jenny hurry past me some time later that afternoon, a worried look on her face, I felt a measure of relief. She, if anyone, would know what had transpired inside the castle.

I intercepted her without hesitation. Her gaze alit on me almost gratefully. "Ah, Master Peddler, you have not seen Farmer Goodman, have you? I am searching him out."

"I did see him, Mistress Jenny, some time back, drinking with his companions and boasting."

Our eyes met with a measure of understanding. She bit her lip. "'Tis true, Master Goodman is a boastful sort of man. A good man, you understand—" She smiled wryly "—as fits his name."

I doubted that.

"But his tongue sometimes does run away with him."

I shrugged. "What's in a name? And," I added, "what has he done with his boasting?"

"Only talked poor Maisie up to the king, to which degree she cannot possibly meet. The poor girl's distraught over it, elated and downcast by turns."

"I do not understand."

"She's elated by the possibility of becoming queen."

My heart fell violently. "How could that happen? Alfred has brought important guests from far and wide in order to choose among them for a wife. He's showing off his kingdom to that purpose."

"Aye, but things do not always go as planned."

That was a truth.

"Poor Maisie can never do what her father has promised. Yet she more than half believes magic will come to her rescue, foolish girl."

"Perhaps it will."

Again, Jenny gazed into my eyes. Without warning, she reached out and seized my wrists. This time, her fingers met my skin, and her touch went through me like a bolt of lightning. Folk so rarely touched me, save by accident.

Now I flinched. Jenny did not seem to notice. "Can you help her? You're full of magic, ain't you?"

"What makes you say that?"

"I can feel it inside you. I can smell it. Will you help her?"

"Help her become queen?" I shook my head.

"That's not how it's meant to be."

"But she's frightened, Master Peddler. If her father will not save her from this madness and you will not, what am I to do?"

"How is it your burden?"

"I told you—she is my friend, my sister in all but blood."

"We cannot save one another, no matter how we try," I told her, thinking of Mallie in her family's clutches, her gaze reaching for mine.

But Jenny's hand tightened on my arm. "Ah, but we can, Master Peddler. That's what love is for."

Chapter Sixteen

Who are we, when it comes down to it? Who was I? No one remembered my name, not by then. I'd been so many things in my life: the babe lying abandoned beneath the cabbage leaf, Ma's son, the rebellious lad seeking to find his way, Mallie's beloved. Since then, all those who lived had forgotten the names Rum and Paul. Jeb knew me as Mr. Stills, Jenny as Master Peddler.

It came to me now that I needed to embrace who I was—become in truth the fae creature I'd always been. Only by doing so could I solve the tangle we were in, and make sure Mallie and I wound up together.

Folk think they know my story from this point on. They describe me as an evil little man, merciless and full of ill-intent, who took advantage of an innocent young girl. Hear the rest of it, and judge for yourself.

After I spoke with Jenny that second time, I went off for a while; I returned to the cottage, where I could be alone with my thoughts, and listen. I supposed Maisie might call on me, and I wanted to be away from the manifold distractions of the fair.

There I sang to myself for comfort, built a fire, and once more searched for answers.

Trust, the fire told me. Trust in the promise.

Ah, well, trust made a difficult proposition for me. I'd trusted Ma, true, but she'd been unable to protect me from Sir's wrath. I'd trusted Mallie, as no other, and she'd been taken from me.

Everyone I loved had been taken from me, and that must mean Jenny, the little brown maid, was wrong. Love was no strength but a weakness.

Was the same thing happening to me now? Having waited so long for Mallie to return to me, would I lose her to her family's wishes once again?

"Tell me," I bade the fire savagely, "or at least show me who—what—I am, that I may save her from this peril. How has her father boasted of her?"

The fire flickered like the skirts of a woman dancing. And then as if feeding on my words, on my wishes, it arose into a mighty pillar.

And showed me.

A dark night. A young woman stumbled down a narrow lane alone, her skirts clutched in both hands. Above her head the stars shone like ice crystals pinned against black fabric, no darker than the color of her hair that tumbled wild and black over her shoulders.

My hair, in both hue and texture.

Shadows cast by the hedgerows flickered across her face; I could not see her as well as I might wish. Then one of the shadows stepped out from the hedge into her path and held out its hand.

A young man. No, he was not. Even as the shadows shifted, so did his form between that of a man and something else, disguised by glamour. I, being what I was, could see through that glamour if I wished—if I dared.

If I truly wanted to know what I was.

I demanded of the fire, of my own power, *Show me.*

It did. He was lithe and slender, with narrow bones like mine and a form not above my height. His face, also narrow, looked quick and clever, no more human than that of a cat. His eyes resembled those of a cat also, deep green and tilted up at the outer corners. He held a grace and a menace, as impossible to describe as to separate the one from the other.

At the sight of him, the girl with the black hair cried out and fell to her knees. She clasped her hands together as if in prayer, though no one ever prayed to such as this.

The creature—the faerie, for let me name him as he was—ignored her reaction and continued to hold out his hand, more demand than invitation.

"Come to me."

"Nay, please leave me. I want you no more."

"You lie, girl. You would never have left your father's cottage and come out this night if you did not want me."

She sobbed, saying, "My flesh may crave you. My soul would keep you away."

The faerie laughed. "Your soul was lost the first time you touched me."

"Have mercy, please. You have already had more than you should of me. Have pity!"

"Pity? Mercy? What are these things? I know them not."

She wept harder, like a woman broken. "But I carry your child."

The faerie laughed again, this time without humor. "You are not the first, nor will you be the last."

"I pray you, use your magic to scourge it from me. Do this, in return for all we have been to one another."

"What have we been, girl?"

"Lovers."

"I do not know what it is to love. I know only the pleasure of your obedience. I care naught for any child."

"If my father finds out, he will beat me."

"Go off somewhere upon the downs, like a rabbit, and bear your child." The faerie waved a hand. "Leave it there to die."

"What kind of mother would so abandon her child?" she cried. "I love it—even if it is part of you."

"That word again. If you care for the child, you will let it die. Such mongrels, gifted with magic, are not welcome in your world."

"Magic? Will my child be gifted with magic?" She thought about that. "Maybe then I *should* leave it to die."

"Come with me." The faerie's voice became a roar, a demand that must be obeyed.

The girl stumbled to her feet, took his hand, and went.

Avid, I watched until the flames died, and then I sagged where I sat. So that was what had begat me, on a young human girl—a soulless being that knew naught of love.

Strange, then, how I wanted to live only to love, and would do anything to have one person devoted to me. My human side coming out, perhaps, my mother's side.

I wondered what had happened to her. Had she done as the faerie bade and lived out on the downs while she carried me? And was that why I felt so much a part of that place, bred and born? And when I at last came into the world, had she left me at the lonely cottage at the edge of the moor, instead of out where no one would find me, out of pity?

What then? Had she gone back to her father's house after all? Had I been raised by Ma and Sir only a few miles distant from her?

Had she ever wondered about me? Or had she perished when the faerie finished with her?

I did not relish being part, blood and bone, of that cold, demanding creature from the vision. But his magic—aye, that I might claim, and it could prove useful to me now.

I let the fire die out, not wanting to see more.

Still and all, if the descendants of the Goodmans still populated the area, there was a chance those of my own half-family did also. Farmer Goodman boasted about being of an old family.

I now knew that, at least on one side, mine proved far, far older—as old as the presence of faeries on the downs. He who would have left me as a newborn out to die, uncaring.

Despite her fear and her loathing, my mother had, at least, been unable to do that. Could there be aught stronger than a mother's protective instinct?

Chapter Seventeen

Did it make me feel more or less ruthless, learning from whence I'd come? To be sure, I'd always known I was at least part fae—Sir had thrown the allegation at me often enough.

Yet knowing for certain did make a difference. Mallie had loved me despite what I was. Could she still?

The vision prompted more questions than it answered. How had they met, the human lass and the heartless faerie? Ma used to say that the wee folks, as she rather innocently called them, were always with us, though we saw them seldom. To be sure, in all my time out on the downs I'd never encountered so much as a solitary brownie. And you'd think, if anyone would, it should be me.

So how had the lass with the black hair met her inarguably ill fate? Was she like me, in that she went wandering the downs whenever she could? Had I inherited that propensity from her, rather than from the merciless being with the eyes as green as my own?

I wanted to shudder every time I thought of him. There's a feeling a person gets—when swallowing a spoonful of cod liver oil, perhaps—a full body grimace, and he made me feel that way.

But he was my father. What did that make me?

She had looked very young, the lass with the black

hair. Young and pretty. So she had strayed over the downs, possibly, and thus encountered him. Perhaps he'd used glamour, even as I did now, in order to disguise himself at the outset and so enchant her. The expression in her eyes argued he attracted even as he repelled her.

She could not help herself.

And where had he gone, after he did his damage and begat me? Had he eventually dropped her? Quite likely, for there had been no feeling in him, even less than Sir, whom I'd always considered hard as granite.

That, however troubling, did not prove to be the aspect which haunted me most. Nay, what possessed my mind was that she had to be a local lass. One just like Mallie, after all, called from the safety of the village by her desire for that vile creature…who'd begat one every bit as vile, and unworthy of love.

I tried to imagine it. When her time—and her pains—took her, she must have gone away onto the downs. I would, myself, have done the same, if I wanted to hide something from Ma or Sir. Had she been able to hide her condition from her family till then? Or had they ordered her out onto the bosom of the moors alone?

Had she, still misguided and half enchanted, gone looking, in her extremis, for him?

Either way, she must have delivered me there— onto the bosom of rock and moss I loved so well. She had not dared take me home and—I still clung to this fact—had not wanted to leave me out there to die.

Why not? She must, by then, have hated him who'd fathered me. I would have been born small and weak. It would have been the easiest of things to leave me for the cold and damp to finish, or even put the palm of her hand over my face and hold it there till I stopped breathing.

It never occurred to me, for all my pondering, that some religious belief might have kept her from that act. But if she hailed from the village, she'd quite likely been schooled at chapel and may have believed such an act to be a sin.

Despite my hard-won cynicism, I found it easier to believe some version of motherly love had kept her from leaving me to die—though save for Ma, I'd never experienced such love. Perhaps, as she did him who'd sired me, she both loved and hated me. Thus, she'd left me in Ma's garden, where I had a chance of being found.

The point was, she must have been on her way back to the village when she deposited me there. But that had been a very long time ago. How was I to discover her identity now?

Why did I still need to discover her identity?

Because a large part of me had gone missing, and even after two hundred years, I wanted it found. Because I could not offer myself fairly to Maisie if I did not understand who I was. Because, having seen my mother in the vision, the idea of her would not let go of me.

I returned from my cottage to the castle grounds, my head buzzing like a hornet's nest. One thing, I decided, lay to my advantage—so many people thronged the place, even at this early hour, no one would take much notice of me, especially with my glamour still in place.

All the way back, I wished. The powers of the land

and sky knew I'd been doing so much wishing of late I fair vibrated with it. But it's as I say, focusing on things—good or bad—brings them to you. I possessed a mind that didn't forget much, but now the intensity of my focus brought a memory to me.

There had been a day long ago—now very nearly lost in the mists of neglected memory—when Ma took me to the market with her. She'd had a number of things she wished to trade, and her back troubled her so sorely by then she did not want to carry it all. I must have been in my early teens and much subject by then to the scorn of the village at large. I never looked forward to market day but in this case had been unable to escape the duty.

Loaded like a pack horse, I followed her down the track over the moor to the village, keeping a wary eye everywhere. Perhaps that is why I noticed him. In truth, we had very nearly finished our business and prepared to head back home when a man passed close by the place we stood.

Something about him caught my attention, the way a glimpse of sunlight through fog might. Some recognition of the blood, perhaps—or so it seemed to me now, in remembering.

He had a wide-brimmed hat pulled well down over his hair, but I could see it was black—black as my own. His was neither a kindly nor a happy face but one deeply scored by lines of what might have been discontent. The set of his shoulders caught my eye, and the shape of his nose.

I drew Ma's attention. "Ma, who is that man?"

She looked up without much interest. "What man?"

"There, wearing the blue shirt."

He'd nearly gone out of sight by then. But I received yet another boon; he paused and turned to speak to someone he passed.

Ma blinked her foggy gray eyes. She no longer saw very well, and for an instant, I didn't think she'd answer. Then she focused on him and studied him hard before turning her gaze on me.

What did I see in her eyes?

Indeed, I believe the emotions there were what set the memory in my mind, because unwanted feelings trembled among the foggy gray. Did she know the man? Did she suspect, then, what I suspected now? Had she wondered about my mother's identity all the while?

The man resumed walking, and I asked once more, urgently, "Who is he?"

"Not sure of his name."

A lie, that. It had to be. Ma had lived here all her life and knew most everyone in the village. Anyway, she did not lie well, not as well as I.

"You must know it."

"Ah—" She pretended to ponder. "Makeswell, I think."

"Makeswell," I repeated.

"Aye."

"And how does Master Makeswell earn his living?"

"Laborer, I believe. He hires out to work other men's land."

I could barely see the back of Master Makeswell by then. He was quite likely too old, anyway, to be my uncle. But another thought occurred to me. "Has he a daughter?"

That captured all Ma's attention. For a long

moment she stared at me. "Why should you ask that?"

I stared back at her and did not answer.

"God's truth, lad, sometimes you scare me, so you do, with your queer ways. Now, come along."

"Has he a daughter?" I insisted.

Ma sucked on her teeth, the few she had left. "He used to, I believe. By name of Rebecca."

"Used to?"

"She's dead."

That struck me, so it did. A shock of surprise passed all the way to my toes. "Dead?"

"So I did hear. Now, come along."

"How did she die?"

"Come—"

"How, Ma?"

"I am not certain, but she's been in the graveyard this long while."

I let it go then. It didn't seem important enough—a passing fancy of a resemblance to a stranger—to keep pushing Ma when she looked to become upset. I tucked the information away into the back of my head, and there it stayed, until this very morning, prompted by last night's vision in the fire.

Now, though, in light of what I'd seen, I wished I had pushed Ma harder back then, when I'd had some chance of discovering more about Rebecca Makeswell. What could I hope to find out about her now, after she'd been two hundred years in the ground?

Strolling through the crowds of onlookers that thronged the castle grounds even at this early hour—some of whom no doubt hadn't seen their beds—one possibility struck me. If she'd gone into the ground some two hundred years ago, she would be there still.

The village might have grown but was not large, and many of the original families had remained. I should be able to find her in the churchyard.

It stood behind the chapel—aye, Reverend Rogers' domain in days of old. I'd always hated the place. Bounded by iron railings on three sides, it never failed to make me feel queasy.

Now, though, I sauntered in, using a stick to lift the latch on the gate so I wouldn't have to touch it with my bare hand. I cast an extra invisibility spell to hide myself, even though those passing by the place, focused on the celebrations, barely gave me any notice.

Aye, it was all about focus.

I do not know how long it took to search the place, the process complicated by the fact that some of the graves, especially the older ones, went without marker stones. At length I found a number of Makeswells, all huddled together. Rebecca did not seem to be among them.

I'm not sure what kept me searching. A grave, even if I found it, would tell me nothing. Yet the search may well not have been for her grave at all. I will tell you something. All human creatures, and some that are not human, crave love—even those who do not entirely believe they deserve it.

I found her at last outside the iron fence, in a group of three or four other neglected mounds, excluded from the churchyard for sins unstated.

Though, in her case, I could guess.

I suppose I was fortunate, in a way; most of these didn't have stones. She did, and her name, Rebecca Makeswell, had been scratched upon it. No dates, but moss coated the back of the stone. She'd probably been dead since I was very young.

I laid the palm of my hand on the ground and tried to summon something, anything, but after the passage of so much time, I came up wanting. She was naught but dust and bone.

Ah, but she'd been banished here—shunned, just like me. It seemed to prove what I suspected and give me an answer I could in no other way attain.

Had she regretted leaving me in Ma's garden? Might she have gone back for me at some point, if she'd lived? Ah, if I could have but one answer, it would be to this question: Why, why did you leave me alive?

Just how strong was a mother's instinct to do absolutely anything for the sake of her child?

Chapter Eighteen

I was not in the best of moods when I returned to the castle grounds, where the fair swiftly built excitement in its third and final day. The search of the graveyard had taken some time; folk now thronged the green sward below the May pole, having come from the village and beyond. Peddlers passed among them, hawking their wares, and a troop of jugglers wandered about, entertaining whoever cared to watch.

Pacing in front of the green just below the castle wall, I observed someone else—a small figure with brown hair and a shawl hanging askew from her shoulders.

She saw me too, and hurried over at once. "Thank heaven you have come."

Not the sort of greeting I usually received, but I returned politely, "Good day, Mistress Jenny."

"'Tis not a good day," she informed me. "Not at all." She waved a hand at the castle. "Maisie has gone in there."

"Into the castle?" My mood immediately worsened still farther. "Why?"

"That is just the thing. She was summoned the moment we arrived. By the king's steward."

"Calm yourself, mistress." I thought to seize her by the arm, even as she had me the day before, but kept from it. "Tell me."

"What do you think I am doing?" Jenny drew a ragged breath. "Her foolish father has bragged on her to the king, saying she is a housekeeper beyond compare. Her! Now, I love Maisie like a sister, but she cannot so much as boil water for tea without scorching it. But Mr. Goodman's boasted that her cakes are lighter than air, her weaving softer than a dream, and her spinning—"

She halted abruptly.

I engaged her eyes. "Aye, Mistress? What of her spinning?"

Agonized, Jenny told me, "He told the king 'tis magical."

"Magical?"

Jenny lowered her voice, causing me to lean closer. "The fool man's only gone and told the king Maisie can spin anything, including straw into gold."

I nearly snorted. The expression in Jenny's eyes kept me from doing so. Instead I asked, "You are not serious?"

"Sadly, I am."

"And the king believes this fabrication?"

"He seems to be every bit as foolish as Master Goodman. He's had Maisie escorted inside, where he expects her to demonstrate her skills." Jenny looked me full in the eyes. "Can you help her?"

I thought hard on it. A delicate balance of wishing and forcing, such a thing would be. I said, "Perhaps. But why should I?"

"Because you are enamored of her." Jenny swallowed. "Most men are."

"What makes you think I am a man?"

This time we gazed at one another long before she said, "You are man enough. I see the way you follow her with your eyes. I fear you are her only hope."

Mallie's only hope—me. Could I possibly make up, in this lifetime, for what had happened in the last, when I failed her?

Jenny added, "And you have the magic. I can feel that much."

I admitted, "I have the magic, aye. But if I am, as you say, enamored of her, if I believe she and I might be destined to be together, why would I then help her impress the king?"

"I don't know." Jenny shivered. "Maybe out of concern? Or—or love?"

I had no answer to that. I'd been chasing love all my life, even if I doubted I deserved it.

That upon which you focus is that which comes true. The truth of it resounded in my mind. All through my time with Mallie, I'd focused on the fear that I might lose her, because I believed I did not deserve such love as hers. What now?

What now?

Jenny stood there watching me while I debated it, her whole heart in her eyes. Jenny, I decided was a good friend to Maisie. A good woman, withal.

"I will think on it," I told her.

"Master Peddler, there is no time now for contemplation. She needs you." She needed me. Ah, perhaps here was the true meaning of our story, come back around.

She needed me.

Only I could save her.

Surely these things should reawaken the love in her heart.

I nodded decisively. "I will go to her."

Now Jenny asked, "How?"

And I gave her a crooked smile. "Just as you say—by magic."

****

Just as well the magic had arisen in me so strongly beside the fire the previous night. I needed it in full. Never before had I attempted anything like transporting from one place to another. I'd learned in the past that my magic depended on both my state of mind and my physical condition. I needed both at peak now.

And I needed a place to be alone, where I would not be disturbed. I found it in a small copse of trees at the edge of the castle grounds, and fortunate I did, for it took me time to settle my mind and my senses, to narrow my focus to Maisie, and make the wish.

Fortunate also that I found her alone when I appeared, for I did so all at once, without warning. Had she been with her father, or the king, or even some servants, I would have been exposed most hideously.

As it was, Maisie started and sprang to her feet when, with an almost audible pop, I entered the chamber where she sat.

In fact, it startled both of us. I regained my composure first, while still she stared at me, her fingers pressed to her mouth and her eyes wide.

I presented her with a small bow. "Mistress Goodman."

"Oh! 'Tis you—the peddler. How do you come here? They've locked the door—however did you get in?"

"Magic." I glanced around the chamber which, barely furnished, contained a stool, a spinning wheel, and a basket full of straw. A single door and a narrow window made for the only openings. "What is this place?"

"We are in the castle. They have put me up in a turret." Her bottom lip trembled, and tears slid down her cheeks, not the first, judging by the tracks I could see already there. "Oh, Master Peddler, what am I to do? They have shut me in here because of all my father's boasting. I told him over and over again not to brag of me, and not to make outrageous promises to the king. Would he listen? And now here am I in this awful fix."

It seemed her father, in this life, was as much the fool as in the last.

"Calm yourself, mistress. Tell me what your father has promised." Though I already knew what Jenny had said.

"You will never believe it. I do not believe it."

"Tell me, or I cannot help you."

She stopped, arrested. "Will you be able to help me?"

"I do not know, do I, until I hear what is required."

"It is mad, entirely. Father wishes for me to wed with the king." She tossed her hands in the air. "Me, a simple farm lass! In order to sway his majesty in our favor, Father told him I can do all sorts of miraculous things."

"Such as?"

"Spin that straw you see there into gold." She pointed a shaking finger at the basket. "If I do not accomplish this ridiculously impossible task by morning, he will punish Father for lying to him. And—and he will punish me also."

She began to weep in earnest, and my heart fair

convulsed in my chest. I had a chance to come to her rescue. Would that allow her to see me as the one she'd once loved?

I went to her and took her hands in mine. "Hush. It will be well. I do think I can help."

"Can you truly?" She stared at me through eyes swimming in tears, blue eyes so like Mallie's it made me ache. "Oh, Master Peddler, if only you can! I will do anything, anything for you in return."

Will you love me as once you did? My desire for it felt so powerful, I had to close my eyes lest she see it.

Reluctantly, I released her hands and bent to examine the straw in the basket. Yellow straw—yellow gold. Aye, given that link, it was possible.

I asked her, "You say this must be accomplished by morning?"

She swiped at her cheeks. "Aye. Oh, Master Peddler, if you can do this thing for me, I will be eternally grateful to you."

Eternally. When it came to her love, I wanted nothing less.

Wish, I told myself.

Gently, I moved her aside and went to sit at the spinning wheel. Ma had taught me to use one, and I had watched her at the task often enough. Now I caressed the curve of the wheel and put my foot to the pedal. Softly, sweetly, it began to turn.

Wish.

I picked up a bit of straw—it changed between my fingers, softened, and became pliable until it transformed into a fine, almost transparent thread, lying across my palm. This I fed into the wheel.

Wish, I told myself for the third time, and called up

all my magic, fueling it with the love I felt for this girl, for whom I'd waited so long. I wished so hard it made me close my eyes.

I heard Maisie's gasp as the golden thread emerged on the other side. Out of sheer gratitude, she wept again.

Chapter Nineteen

"Everyone is talking about it, and naught else," Jenny said anxiously, her gaze seeking mine. "Mr. Goodman is fair beside himself."

A new day had dawned. After working Maisie's miracle for her, I'd transported back out of the tower room and returned to my cottage, feeling shaken and spent.

I will admit I had doubts about what I'd done. By spinning that basket of straw into gold for Maisie, had I enabled her to secure the king's interest? Had I damaged my own chances?

Yet she'd needed me. I'd been the only one who could save her. That must count for something.

The desire to learn what had come of my deed made me drag myself back to the castle grounds sleepless, foodless, and still feeling drained. Jenny must have been watching for me, for she ran to me at once.

"Aye," I admitted. "I heard folk speaking, on my way here." Gossiping with avid interest.

I seized hold of Jenny's arms, to steady myself, and she blinked at me. "Master Peddler, are you well?"

I did not think so—I feared I'd pushed myself where I should not go. But the die had been cast and there was no calling it back now.

"Has she been released from the tower?" I asked. "Was Maisie freed?"

"Aye."

Then I was well enough. "Where is she?"

"At home, resting."

"Do you think she will mention that 'twas I did the spinning for her?" That point had worried me most the night. At parting, I'd warned Maisie to keep my presence in the tower room secret. Still sobbing in gratitude, she'd agreed. But it occurred to me she might let something slip while trying to explain how she'd accomplished her miracle, and that could be the worse for me. The king had promised to deal harshly with Goodman, and with Maisie also, if they were proved to have lied to him. How might he deal with me?

Was he the sort of man to hunt down a faerie known to be loose in his kingdom? He believed in magic, aye, yet folk were unpredictable. Such thoughts had kept me from sleep, despite my exhaustion.

"I do not suppose she will be so foolish as to admit the talent that turned straw into gold was not hers alone," Jenny said wryly. "Besides, who would believe it? That she was able to summon you, I mean, and that once summoned you would agree to perform such a miracle for her." She lowered her voice carefully. "The room was locked. And by any road, why should a faerie be at her command?"

Why, indeed. No one—not even Maisie—knew how I loved her, that I had loved her unstintingly for two centuries. I'd hoped, once I helped her, she would see me for who I was, but though overcome with gratitude, she'd regarded me no differently.

"I need to see her," I said, more to myself than to Jenny.

"Impossible. Her parents have her bunged up in the

farmhouse, talking of the future and what she can, and cannot, do."

"The future?" For an instant I wavered, focusing on unwanted things.

"Here." Now Jenny seized my forearms in turn, steadying me. "When is the last time you took anything to eat?"

"I don't rightly recall."

"Come with me."

Only a few vendors did business so early; Jenny towed me over to one and purchased two meat pies. We sat side by side in the shelter of a hedgerow while the day grew around us, and she assured I ate every bite.

"There. Sit—I will be back in a moment."

I watched her cross the green grass, her brown skirt gathering dew. When she returned, she brought a pot of ale, which she put in my hand.

"There, drink. All of it."

Instead I asked, "What am I to do? I have made a terrible muddle of this."

Jenny stared away over the grass a long moment and made no answer.

At length she said, "You have performed Maisie a great service."

"I have made her more desirable to the king."

"True enough. But she is very grateful to you. She poured her heart out to me about that, though she dares not speak your name." Jenny smiled wryly. "Well, she does not know your name, not your true name, but you know what I mean."

Maisie—Mallie—should recall my name. She should know me. Oh, what would it take to make her remember?

"Do you think it is done?" I asked Jenny. "Do you think the king will now leave her be?" Might we begin meeting on the downs again? Might I sing for her, breathe for her, live for her?

"No. I do not think the king will leave her be." Jenny glanced at me. "She says that before you left the tower room you reminded her she might call on you again, by grasping that pendant you gave her and wishing."

"Aye."

"Is it truly so easy as that, Master Peddler? Need a lass merely wish, in order to win your company?"

That snagged all my attention. I gazed into her eyes and for an instant saw there the mist floating across the downs, the light of the world strengthening over the land, all reflected in the flicker of a speckled trout's side.

I did not understand what she asked of me, and said nothing.

She sighed. "Drink your ale," she bade me, and so I did.

****

Promises are easily given, and far less easily kept. This is a thing I have learned, to my sorrow. Words have power because they are connected to emotions. Wishes have such power, as does love. But for a promise spoken to hold true, it must be given in truth.

Mallie had never lied to me; she never would. Her words and feelings—her heart—remained true always.

I offer that as an excuse for what happened next. I believed Maisie to be Mallie, and I did not think Mallie would ever seek to go back on a promise to me.

The call came at the beginning of the evening

when, still exhausted, I'd just gone to my rest. I'd spent hours with Jenny, as the third and final afternoon of the fair got underway, only to see Maisie arrive in a train that included her parents, all decked out in finery. They were admitted to the castle with considerable fanfare.

Though Jenny and I had been standing by, Maisie did not so much as glance at me.

Even though I wished it.

I will admit I felt a chill of foreboding then. I am not completely the fool, though admittedly my tale must argue for it. Desire has a power all its own.

No sooner had sleep claimed me that night than its soft darkness split, cleaved by a light so bright it seared my mind.

Help. Help me!

I could feel it, so I swear, feel her hand on the pendant stone, clutching, her mind calling to mine, her raw desperation.

I lay staring into the darkness of the tiny bedroom, for I'd long since traded my berth in the loft for its far more ordinary comforts. The spell I'd put on the pendant compelled me, as did my love for her. I barely had time to don the glamour that disguised me before I transported to the tower room.

The same room.

Yet this time it looked and felt crowded. Maisie still stood there alone, with only her stool and spinning wheel for company. But piles and piles of straw surrounded her.

"Oh, thank heaven you have come!" she cried when I appeared, seeming too desperate for surprise. "I held onto the pendant, as you said, and called and called for you. I need your help."

She'd been weeping again—I could see the marks on her exquisite face. Apart from that, she looked different. She wore a fancy gown, made of fabrics green and gold, such as no farm lass ever owned, and her hair had been dressed up on top of her head, piled high, making her look far less like my Mallie, the half-wild girl of the downs.

I asked, "What is all this?"

She waved her hands frantically. "As you see! The king, it seems, proves a greedy man. Not satisfied with what we did for him, spinning a single basket of straw to gold, he has now given me this task, a whole room full of straw. Oh, what am I to do?"

I observed the room with considerable dismay, and my heart sank.

"He says he will marry me," she went on wretchedly, "if I can accomplish this feat. I will then have proved myself worthy, you see."

"Do you wish to marry the king?"

"I don't know, do I? It's mad, all of it. For me—me, a village lass—to become a queen, well, who would not want that?"

You are meant to be mine.

"Yet how can I be queen? I know nothing of holding such a place. Still, 'tis better than death."

"Death?"

She gazed at me with stark, distracted eyes. "He says if I fail in this, he will know Father and I have deceived him. He will seize Father's farm as punishment for lying. My entire family will suffer for Father's folly. And I—" She gulped. "He says he will sentence me to death."

Death. I saw her again in her family's clutches,

drawing her last breath.

"Can you help me, Master Peddler?"

"I do not know." Again, I gazed around the room, my eyes measuring the billowing piles of straw. The last feat had depleted me dangerously. I didn't think I had power enough for this.

But she'd called on me, she depended on me. Even while I hesitated, she came and seized my fingers. She sank into the pile of straw at my feet and pressed her forehead to my hands. "Oh, please, Master Peddler. Save me! You are my only hope. Save my family, please."

I could feel her trembling.

Bitterly I said, "I care naught for your family." I hated them all, with the exception of Jenny, not related to Maisie by blood so much as by sentiment. "But I do care about you."

I love you. I need you.

"Perhaps we can bargain," I told her slowly.

"Aye. Aye, Master Peddler. Do this for me and I will make you any promise you ask, in return. Once I am queen I can give you great riches. A fine house, perhaps. Whatever you wish."

The word fell artlessly from her lips. *Wish, wish, wish.*

I want you. But I couldn't say that, not outright. Standing before her she saw a wizened little man—not he whom she'd once loved. She still did not know me. She, who knelt there beseeching me with Mallie's eyes.

Nay, I needed to be far more devious than to just ask it outright.

"What else can I do? Do you truly suppose I will have a choice? Father will push me to it if—if—" She nodded at the piles of straw again.

Just like Jules Longford, I thought bitterly. The past, the dark and terrible past, repeated itself.

"What makes you think, if I wreak this miracle for you, the king will not merely demand an even greater room spun, and after that another?"

"Would all this, once spun, not be enough for anyone?"

I did not know.

"Get up," I bade her.

She stumbled to her feet, one of her hands still clutching mine, raw hope in her eyes. I knew then I would help her, even if it cost me my life, even if it cost me her company. Such was my love for her.

Yet the cunning side of me, the faerie side, insisted I must pin her down somehow. Win something for myself.

I squeezed her fingers hard. "I want your word, Maisie Goodman, if I do this thing for you, I will have your loyalty in return."

"My loyalty, aye." For an instant her eyes went wide. "What, just, does that mean?"

"You will remain my friend and any promises you give to me will be true."

"I can agree to that. 'Tis an easy thing."

"Nay, it is the hardest of things."

If she wed the king, everything would change. She would dress in finery every day, would have no need of magic or the little man who'd helped her. I saw that, even as I saw I could do nothing other than spin that straw into gold. She might become his wife, but she would remain forever mine, mine, *mine*.

"Say you will still see me, meet with me on the

downs, sit and talk with me." So little to ask, in return for much. "A sacred promise, mind."

"I do so promise."

"The first Sunday of each month you will come to me, where the old shepherd's hut did stand."

I still clutched her fingers. They spasmed in my grip like a bird trying to escape a snare.

But her pink lips, so like rose petals, parted. She said, "I do so promise. Can you do it, Master Peddler? Can you spin all this straw into gold before dawn?"

Chapter Twenty

It cost me dear, that feat of magic. I pushed my innermost abilities as never I had before, not when I made songs for her and sang them sweetly in some sunny dell, not when I went to her father's house to fight for her. I was, after all, but half faerie. The human side of me suffered that night, and by the time the first rays of light came over the stone sill of the tower window, I was beyond spent.

"Clever fellow, you have done it!" crowed she who had watched me spin for a time before curling up in a corner and going to sleep. Curiously, she'd awakened only when my wheel at last stopped turning, when every scrap of wishing had drained from me, and my fingers ached too sorely for me to bend them.

I arose from my back-breaking position on the stool. Did I have the strength necessary to transport out?

But she pushed at me. "Quickly, you must go. It is nearly daylight! They will come and find you here."

"You will remember your promise?"

"I will, aye."

I looked her in the eye. "You will keep it?"

"Have I not said? Oh, by heaven, I hear footsteps on the stairs. Will you not go?"

I went, and once more the waiting began.

****

I had thought myself patient, before, when I passed two centuries awaiting her. I'd possessed her promise, after all, given me from her dying lips, and I'd had perfect faith in her. Now, though, all my patience seemed flown. Being in her company again—knowing that the togetherness for which I'd yearned lay nearly within my grasp—destroyed what tolerance I'd earned. I wanted her to come to me. I wanted her to know me, so my life could begin again.

But 'twas not to be so easy as that.

Very soon after the second night we passed in the turret room together, news of a wedding issued from the castle, announced to all. The king, perhaps anxious for that elusive heir or perhaps only anxious to make Maisie his own, did not drag his feet. A mere three weeks later, they were wed.

It proved a grand state affair, far more dignified than the fair, and I watched from a distance with my hat pulled well down over my eyes. When Maisie arrived in a gilded carriage with her train of maidens, I numbered but one in the crowd. A member of Maisie's train, so I saw, at the very end, was little brown Jenny.

It had gone hard with me, recovering from that night of spinning. For days, I'd been flat on my back, neither eating nor drinking. And it pained me sorely to see her go to her wedding with another. Truly, I felt close to despair then. But, so I told myself, such vows as she gave to the king must be empty things. She might not be able to escape marriage to him, but her heart remained mine.

I had only to convince her to remember. And that, so I assured myself repeatedly, would occur when she kept her promise and came to me.

On the day—the first Sunday of the next month—I was at the site of the old shepherd's hut early. Little remained of the place these days, just an outline of the foundation, ridges in the stone, and an aura I fancied I alone could feel.

I paced, I talked to myself, I even sang for a time. Sunday, I acknowledged, might be a difficult day for her to come. She might be required to attend chapel with her new husband.

But she owed me. I had done much for her, and asked little in return.

When, just before noon I saw a woman's form coming toward me across the moor, I went breathless with anticipation and delight. I'd been right to keep faith with her, right to forge the connection between us with that feat of magic. And even if I had her company for only one day a month, that was worth all.

Disappointment did not find me till she drew near enough for me to see her clearly. Then I noticed how the sun lit her hair, not to gold but a warm, nut brown. No curls, but a smooth crown twisted into plaits, and a pair of speckled brown eyes, full of regret.

Anger came flooding swiftly on the heels of the disappointment. Not anger at Jenny, no; she had no fault in any of it. But seeing her there in Maisie's place came hard.

"Good day to you, Master Peddler," she said when she reached me.

I made no reply, unable to speak.

Her lips twisted in a wry smile. "I know I am not she whom you hoped to see. But I did not want to leave you here waiting, and waiting."

I nearly choked when I said, "You know about our

agreement, then?"

"Maisie told me. She tells me most things. Come." She touched me lightly on the arm. "Let us sit and talk."

My heart rebelled. I did not want to sit and talk with Jenny. I had been longing without cease for what I thought would occur this day. Still, it had been kind of her to walk out all this way, and folk did not do such things for me often enough that I could shrug it off.

We sat side by side on a moss-covered ridge that used to be part of the hut's foundation.

She glanced at me. "What you did for Maisie that night, spinning a room full of straw into precious gold—do not mistake, she is grateful."

"Then she should have kept her promise, and come."

Jenny flapped her hands helplessly before she said, "'Twas impossible. She is newly wed. There are demands on her."

"What sort of demands?"

"The king rarely lets her out of his sight."

I did not like the way that made me feel, not at all. I scowled. "She sent you to make her excuses?"

Jenny remained silent so long I turned my head and looked at her. "She did not send you."

"'Tis as I say, it haunted me thinking of you here, waiting with no word. So—so I came."

I spoke a bitter word under my breath.

"I know, Master Peddler, it is scarcely an acceptable substitution. My company is not hers, and never will be. But I thought—you are lonely, as am I. We might be friends."

"Lonely?" The word did not come any closer to

what I felt than a marsh light comes to the burning sun.

Jenny bit her lip and remained silent a long moment. "I understand you love her. I am, as I say, a poor substitute."

"She made me a promise."

"And will keep it, I do not doubt, next month when she finds herself better able."

"Do you believe so?" I could scarcely warrant how my heart yearned for it.

"I do. But give her time to find her feet."

"I detest folk who do not keep their promises."

"As do I, Master Peddler."

"I want her to remember me."

"Aye, indeed. She owes to you her new position, her welfare and that of her father. I will remind her."

"She should not need reminding."

Jenny got to her feet. "You do not wish for me to stay. I will walk back now."

"Wait." I put out a hand to keep her. For an instant, the specks in her eyes brightened.

"Aye?"

"Take Mallie a message for me. Tell her she made me a promise. Warn her not to miss next month's meeting."

Jenny frowned. "Mallie? Who is Mallie?"

"I meant Maisie." I also rose. "One more thing you may tell me. Is she well?"

The brightness in Jenny's eyes dimmed, though she said, "Very well."

I nodded. That, above all else, mattered. "Thank you, Mistress Jenny. 'Twas a kindness in you, to walk so far for so little."

This time her smile looked tight. "No trouble at all,

in my soul withered and died; rage arose to take its place.

The Sunday of the month after that, one of pinching cold and intermittent sleet, Jenny once more walked out the long way from the village. She came wrapped in a cloak of deep green, but nevertheless did not deceive me, this time, as to her identity.

She approached the site of the shepherd's hut and stood looking at me for many moments without words before she at last said, "Master Peddler, how do I find you? Are you well?"

An interesting question. I felt battered; I felt torn. I had—as when Mallie died—once more transformed into someone I barely recognized.

Bitterly, I said, "That is not my name."

"I know." The light in those brown eyes of hers flickered at me. "I have been asking about you, all around the district. 'Tis said your name is Stills— Master Stills, is all anyone can say. Peddler was just what you became in order to get close to Maisie."

Funny how much of it she seemed to understand. "Aye."

"We need to speak together. Come walk with me. 'Tis too cold to sit here."

"What have we to discuss?"

She didn't answer, merely set a course northwestward across the moor. We went in silence for a time, over the hoary ground and through the mist-stilled air, before she said, "Beautiful place, this. Lovely, the way a tune is lovely, one you've nearly forgotten. Haunting."

That made me give her a sharp look indeed. "Haunting, aye, mistress, and it will destroy you, if you let it."

"I am not so easily destroyed, Master Stills. And I can see through you. Through that magic you wear, I mean. You are not so aged-looking as you would have us believe."

"I am, in fact, very ancient."

"Your hands are those of a young man, and you have no lines at the corners of your eyes. You try to disguise your hair with streaks of white, but it is very black. Your limbs are lithe."

Ruefully, I asked her, "How is it you have always been able to see through me?"

"I do not know. Maybe because we are two of a kind, a bit lost in this world. Folk look at us and see what we are not but fail to see what we are. Neither of us belongs."

"Perhaps so."

"Tell me, Master Stills, what do you see when you look at me? The shy mouse of a housemaid?"

"No," I admitted wryly.

"The plain little spinster-in-waiting?"

"I think if you wanted a husband, you would have one."

"Do you, so?" That made her raise a brow. "Even if the one I wanted did not turn his gaze toward me?"

Ah, and I knew how that felt. "He would be a fool indeed, mistress, who looked yet did not see you."

That made her laugh. The sound chimed like bells over the frozen downs. How long since a lass's laughter had sounded here?

"What's funny?" I asked.

"Oh, naught—naught but that I thought you a clever man. 'Tis one of the things I admired about you."

"You speak in riddles."

"Do you not like riddles?"

I did; I always had. But Jenny was a riddle in female form.

"Why have you come?" I asked her. "To tell me Maisie will not be keeping her promise? I think I am clever enough to have figured that."

"Yet I find you here, waiting." She looked suddenly grave. "It breaks my heart that you wait, yet no one comes. I merely determined that today, someone should."

"Again, you show me more kindness than I deserve."

"Who are you, Master Stills, to decide what you deserve?"

I gave a harsh laugh. "Who else is there?"

"Me, perhaps."

"If you will do something for me, bring Maisie here. What is her excuse this time?"

"She is expecting a child."

The admission hit me in the gut with the impact of a hard blow. "Is she, indeed? Ah, and must that put an end to that which she promised me?" Did it matter to me? Nay, for I loved her still. Pain caused me to say, "Whatever the reason, she needs to be punished for breaking her promise."

"Does she?"

"Aye."

We'd reached the place for which she'd apparently been making, one of the old kistvaens, or stone tombs, that pepper the downs. I'd sat here so often with Mallie in the past, singing songs and talking nonsense, it seemed odd to be here with someone else now.

She lowered herself onto the stone curb, ignoring the dusting of snow, and I joined her. The wind cut a bit less cold here, and the two of us might have been alone in the world.

But no, for my pain still accompanied me.

"How do you mean to punish Maisie?" Jenny asked after a while.

A good question. She had forgotten me, quite plainly—gone about the life I'd helped her achieve and dismissed me, and her promise, from her mind.

Almost to myself I said, "She needs a visit, and reminding."

"You will never get near her. Alfred keeps her very much to himself, since the marriage. She hasn't even been back to the farm."

"I can get in."

She turned her head and looked at me. "Ah, to be sure you can. But should someone see you, it could prove very dangerous for you, indeed."

Grimly, I said, "Only one person will see me. Anyway, do you suppose me powerless, that I cannot defend myself?"

"I do not suppose that at all. But Alfred is powerful also, and has many men he might send to hunt you down." Jenny drew a breath. "I only wish…"

The word hung on the frosty air between us, and made me seek her gaze. Did she comprehend the potential of wishing, this brown hen of a lass who, I began to see, was anything but plain? Did she know a wish could steer the current of a life, and turn the world?

"What do you wish, mistress?"

"That, perhaps, I were the one you loved with all

your heart."

With those words, she leaned in and kissed me. We sat shoulder to shoulder; she did not need to lean far. But it might have been the distance of centuries.

So long had it been since I so much as felt the hand of another. This—this! Her lips felt soft and warm despite the chill of the air around us. I could taste—

A hint of sweetness, a hint of wildness. The suggestion of who she was. But she withdrew from me almost before it began, like someone who opens a door and, fearing to see what lies within, slams it shut again.

She scrambled to her feet in a flurry of brown skirts and, having given me a single look from those brown-speckled eyes, ran.

I did not call after her. I believe I was too stunned. I did not follow after her, either, even though the warmth of that kiss seemed to travel through me like a blessing.

I remained far too focused on the hurt within.

Chapter Twenty-Two

I planned it properly this time. No rushing into a chamber well-guarded or where the new queen might not be on her own. I sent my thoughts ahead of me, searching. I located the room she most often occupied at night, learned her spiritual signature so I could tell if she was there alone.

All the while, my anger simmered. I wanted to hurt Maisie, even as she'd hurt me. I did not see the truth of that then, though I do now. Perhaps my feelings obscured my true motives from me.

Because I still loved her, and I believed her to be not so much disinterested as mistaken. For I knew Mallie's heart, and believed if only she once recognized me, everything would change.

My power had grown considerably since I first visited the turret room and spun straw to gold. Here is a secret I will share with you: the ability for magic increases in the using. I had pushed myself to my limits and beyond, the last time I saw Maisie. Whatever talent lay within me, it had responded to and met that demand.

I chose, so, a night when I knew the king was away on a state visit. Oh, aye, I could tell when he was with her; those nights tore at my heart. But this evening, deep within the winter's chill and silent as the watching stones, he remained far away.

So did I gather power, clothe myself in a measure

of glamour, and transport on a swift current of magic to where she was. This night I meant to reveal my identity to her—drop the glamour and show her who I truly was.

The room in which I arrived, as far different from the barren turret room as could be, afforded every comfort. Fine, crimson draperies hung at the windows and a thick, patterned carpet lay over the cold floor. The bed, which sat high on a platform to one side, had been turned down for the night, but no one yet occupied it.

Instead, Maisie sat snug beside the fire, which burned brightly on a hearth as tall as she. And, ah, the sight of her froze me where I stood.

She wore a robe of deep blue over a myriad of ruffles, and her hair hung loose like a river of gold—so much like the straw I'd spun, in fact, it made me catch my breath. Her rose-petal face looked pensive, but when I appeared it altered at once into an expression of alarm.

"You!" she gasped, and leaped to her feet.

How can I describe my feelings then? I'd longed to see her. I'd ached from her treatment of me. Love and spite tangled so closely in my heart, I could no longer tell them apart.

"Good evening, mistress."

Her lips worked, though for a moment no words emerged. She darted a look at the door—I stood between her and escape—and another at the window. "How did you get in?" she gasped then.

"By magic. By use of the very magic you sought from me. Did you forget?"

Forget, forget…how could you forget me, Mallie? How, when we were everything to one another, when I would have traded the world and everything in it for your sake?

She shook her head wildly. Her hair flowed around her; she looked impossibly beautiful.

I moved a step closer. "You and I, mistress, had a bargain."

"I know."

"I agreed to spin all that straw into gold for you, at a very modest price. I asked only that you give me one day a month in your company."

"I know," she said again. "I do so recall. But—but, Master Peddler, everything has changed since then." She lifted her head proudly. "Perhaps you have not heard, but I have become queen. And—and I carry the king's child."

"I did hear."

"So how could I—how could I go haring off to the downs, to meet a—a—" She waved a hand at me.

"A what, mistress?"

"A boggart, or a brownie, or whatever you may be."

"You had no quarrel with what I might be when you used me to your own end."

"I did. I assure you, kind sir, I did. But I was in a spot of sore difficulty, was I not? Truly desperate." Ready tears flooded her lovely eyes. "Surely you recall how desperate I was."

I will admit, I hated her then. At that moment, my hatred passed through me so sharp and immediate, it felt like the thrust of an iron sword. All the spite of my father's folk coursed through me in response. I almost—almost—forgot I also loved her.

"I recall," I assured her in a voice that sounded

nothing like my own. "It changes nothing. You made a promise to me, did you not?"

"I did."

"Promises are sacred things."

I could see, in her wide, tear-washed eyes, how her thoughts raced like a mouse trapped by a cat, with no escape.

"I do know that, Master Peddler. But surely you see how everything has conspired against me keeping that promise. It is not possible for me to meet you as you have asked. 'Twould be a betrayal of my husband, first of all."

And what of her betrayal of me? My heart cried the question, but she could not hear.

"So you have no intention of keeping the promise you gave me."

She shook her head once more.

"What of all the straw I spun into gold for you? Should I turn it back to straw once again?"

She paled. "Then Alfred would want to know what happened. He would think my magic faulty. He would ask me to do it all over again. He would believe me false." She thought about that for an instant. "You would not be so cruel."

"No? What of your cruelty in leaving me to wait for you, over and over again?"

"I—I did not see it that way. What can it possibly mean to you, whether or not I keep some meeting? We scarce know one another."

Hearing that, I knew I had to make her see me, make her recognize me at last. I lifted both hands in front of my face, spread the fingers and dissolved my glamour.

She screamed. Recoiling violently, she withdrew what little of herself she'd extended to me.

Hurt rushed through me, insupportable. As usual, anger hurried in to fill the hole it made. Even as she gasped, I said, "You must be punished for betraying me."

"What are you? Who—"

Who. She knew me not, she knew me not!

I told her viciously, "I can cause you to lose your place here, with but a wave of my hand."

"Please, no. I am to have a child."

"I can make the king see you for the liar you are."

"But I love him!"

She loved him, not me.

"Be merciful, Master Peddler. So I do beseech."

Mercy? She asked for mercy?

"You will pay for breaking your promise, one way or another. Either I expose you—"

"Nay, please!"

"Or you must give me your child once it is born."

She paled still further before flushing red. Her hands flew to her belly. "My child? What should you want with my child?"

I did not want the child. The powers knew, I would have no idea what to do with it. But if my own history had taught me one thing, it was about the power of attachment between a mother and child. Even my own mother, who both feared and hated my father, had refused to take me out upon the moor and strangle me. Instead, she'd left me where I had a chance of being rescued.

Maisie's child, so I figured, was the one thing that might bring her to me, if I held possession of it. The child was the one thing that might mean more to her than the greedy, coercive king. If it rested in my hands, she would come to me.

"You owe me," I told her, and believed it.

She whispered, stricken, "I cannot give up my child."

"Then as soon as the king returns home, you shall stand exposed for the liar and deceiver you are."

See me, my heart whispered still. *See me*.

She clasped her hands together.

She wept.

I stood unmoved.

"Do not take our child, please! Our firstborn." She fell to her knees. "I will promise you anything else."

"How can I trust any promise you give me?" How, since she'd lied to me? "I must have the child to hold, so I may assure you do as I say."

"Oh, mercy, oh, mercy," she repeated. She gazed into my eyes, and seeing no mercy there climbed back to her feet.

"Do not expose me, vile faerie," she breathed. "Do not, and you shall have the child."

Chapter Twenty-Three

Those who have told and retold the story usually pause at this point and ask, "How could any mother give away her child?"

Few bother to ask how I could demand it. In the tales, I am considered a foul creature indeed, dark, twisted, and capable of any evil. They do not wonder what a boggart or a brownie might want with a human child. Its only purpose, as I tell you now, was to bring her to me.

Because, by all the powers of the earth and the sky, by the blessed downs themselves, I needed her still. I wanted Mallie back and believed I could at length force Maisie to see me.

So I went away and waited, waited as I had before, this time for the child to be born. During that time—some six months—Jenny did not approach me. I could only imagine what she, who I fancied had held me in some favorable regard, who had kissed me with affection, must think of me now.

No worse than what I thought of myself. I had doubts about the course of action I'd chosen, yet even as the time crawled by, I could think of no other way to force Maisie's compliance. My anger and sense of betrayal, twined together, fair burnt me up.

Then came a day in late May when Jenny did come walking out to see me. Rafts of tall, puffy clouds chased through a sky of aching blue, and warmth stole over the land, teasing the tiny flowers into bloom. The downs lay patched in gray, yellow, and green, and my heart yearned, yearned.

I do not know how Jenny found me. She never seemed to have much difficulty doing so. This time she located me at the edge of my own land, gazing away over the place I loved so dearly.

She came up and stood at my shoulder with the tail of her hair streaming in the wind, gazing afar, as did I, and said nothing.

"Have you news for me, Mistress Jenny?"

"The babe is born."

"Ah."

We stood on so in silence for some while before she said, "Do you not mean to ask is it lad or lass?"

"It makes no difference to me."

She did stare then. I could feel the impact of those brown-specked eyes even though I did not meet them.

"'Tis a wee lass, and beautiful. It was a healthy, if difficult, birth."

"So?"

"Maisie does not wish to part with the child. She sent me to find you, to beg a reprieve. Master Stills, this is your chance to show mercy, to prove the worth of your heart."

I laughed. "What is the worth of my heart, then? Can you tell me?"

"I believe so. I have continued asking about you around the district, all winter long. It seems you have lived here as far back as anyone can remember, yet you are not aged, though you do your best to appear so. No one knows your name, save 'Master Stills.' "

"There is one who knows my name. She must yet remember."

"Is that what all this is about? You want something from Maisie, something she cannot give."

"She could, if she would. She must remember."

"Master Stills, how could she remember you, when you only just met before the fair? She is a new wife, and happy with her husband and child. Aside from the threat you have leveled on the babe, you mean nothing to her."

Nothing, nothing.

"I think she would love Alfred even were he not king."

I doubted that.

"Master Stills, one cannot choose where love may alight."

True.

"Why will you punish her this way? A child needs its mother."

"She may see her child whenever she wishes. All she needs do is come to me."

"Ah, so you will hold that innocent babe hostage to your love?"

"If that is what it takes."

Jenny fell silent again. For many moments we stood so, shoulder to shoulder, with the sweet wind off the downs buffeting us. Then she said, "Have you thought about the fact that a love you must coerce and force into being is no real love at all?"

That made me pull my eyes at last from the far distance and turn to look at her. She gazed back at me, the trouble in her eyes rampant, her small, round face distressed.

I remembered again, suddenly, the feel of her lips on mine. But I said, "Mistress Jenny, look at me."

"I am looking."

"What do you see? I am a half human, no more than that. He who sired me on a human lass—and he a user, no doubt, like all his kind—has long disappeared back into his faerie mound. Even though I believe a mother's love to be the strongest on earth, my mother could not stand to raise me and abandoned me in a garden. I have but one chance for love—one. If that were true of you, Mistress Jenny, would you not fight for that chance? Would you not cheat and risk all for it? I coerce nothing. She already loves me—the only lass who ever has, or ever will."

Jenny drew a long breath and light flickered in her eyes. "You do not think you deserve love."

"It came to me once—once—against all odds. I will do anything to retain it. Go to her, remind her she made a promise to me, and this one she will keep."

"Mercy—"

My lips twisted bitterly. "Out of mercy, I will give her three days with her child. Three nights from now, I will come for the babe."

"And if she is guarded, being forewarned? If she is not alone—"

"Do you forget? I have magic on my side." I turned away then, unable to face what I saw in Jenny's eyes. "Tell her also I am disappointed in her. The lass that once I knew would never have lied to me."

"As you are desperate enough to coerce, she is desperate enough to lie."

But, my heart insisted, the love remained true. So it must be—without that belief, I had nothing.

****

Those three days passed the slowest of all. I walked far over the downs, soaking up the spring sunshine, but the fine weather proved no real distraction. I tended my stills and hauled a load of homebrew off to the coast. I sat for endless hours beside the fire where I once more saw images of Mallie holding a babe in her arms.

I wondered what Jenny had told her of me. Jenny, a curious little creature, perhaps knew more of me than anyone else left alive. But she'd taken Maisie uncompromising news, and I doubted she'd seek to soften it.

Did I wonder what I—a half man—would do with a newborn once I had it? I knew nothing of infants. Yet I could see the parallels between me and that child, despite the differences in our gender and circumstance.

As Ma had cared for me, I would so care for it.

I'll admit, I hoped Maisie would come to me before times, without involving the child, and agree to the association I'd already requested—a friendship, the sharing of company. She did not, so I marshaled my strength and my magic, and on that third night once more invaded her chamber at the castle.

Forewarned, this time she'd made preparations. She had two guards stationed outside the door, but I did not need to use the door. Any other woman, sore afraid, might have made sure her husband occupied the room with her. She—with her own deception weighing on her mind—dared not. Only the babe was there, lying in a wicker cradle all decked with pink ribbons.

Maisie wore pink also, a color that suited her right well. A robe of lace and ruffles spilled over her arms and swept the floor when she spun, in alarm, to face me. She'd rarely looked more beautiful.

"You!" she breathed as she had before—even though she must have been expecting me. "Be gone! Leave at once—there are guards outside the door, and I will scream."

"Go ahead and try. There is a spell of silence fast around this chamber. They'll not hear you."

"My husband—"

"He won't hear you either." Alfred, as I could easily sense, occupied the next room, and lay fast asleep. "Besides, if you bring him in here, he will then learn of your perfidy, will he not?"

Agony flooded her clear blue eyes. "Perhaps 'twould be best. I cannot go on this way."

"You will then lose everything, instead of just your babe."

"How can you be so cruel? Jenny speaks much of you. She tries to make excuses, says you do what you do for the sake of love. But how can you expect love from me? Look at you. Who could love what you are?"

Those words cut me deep. They fair threatened to flay me. They made me blurt, "You did, once."

"Ha!" She stared. "Impossible."

"It is true," I assured her. "You have merely forgotten. If you would but once come to me—out there on the downs where we used to meet, where we meant everything to one another, then you would see."

She shook her head. "You are mad. I love my husband and my child." She went and gathered up the babe from the basket, most carefully. Cuddling it to her, she began weeping prodigiously. "You cannot take her."

"Then leave her here and come you away with me. Give me but one night—"

"A whole night? With you?"

"Aye." I would sing to her, tell her the old stories, at last make her remember me.

She wavered, and for an instant I actually believed I'd won. I held out my hand to her.

But the agony in her eyes transformed to something else, and she gave a low, hysterical laugh. "I will go nowhere with you, foul creature."

"Then the child is mine."

"Nay, please!"

"Maisie, you will keep a promise made to me, and it shall be this one."

"Mercy!" She wept in earnest. Her gaze, softened by tears, clung to mine. "Do not take her. Do not expose me. Give me one more chance."

Why did I agree? Was it the love for the child I saw in her eyes? The wish that such love might once more be directed at me?

Wish.

I told her, "Aye, I will give you your chance. I will return to you each of the next three nights. If you can remember me and speak my name—my full, true name—you may keep the child."

"Remember you?"

"My name." She alone in the world remained who would know it. "I will appear here at the same time each night. If you cannot speak my true name by the third night, you will keep your word and give that child into my keeping."

"Aye, aye. Surely I will be able to guess it."

"Not guess—know," I warned her.

"Indeed, that is what I meant. Now go, before my husband hears."

"Do you truly suppose he loves you?" I leaned close and asked it, just before I disappeared from the chamber. "Not so much as I do."

Chapter Twenty-Four

Maisie must have sent Jenny everywhere that next day, asking after me. Trouble was, Jenny had already asked anyone who might possibly know me, and no one left alive remembered my name.

Joe and Jeb's descendants might know me as Master Stills, aye. One of them might even come up with my first name, if pressed. No one knew the whole of it: Rum Paul Stillskin.

I tramped far that day, across the downs, trying to lose my anxious emotions in the beauties of the place I loved. When I returned to the farm at nightfall, Jenny waited there for me.

She sat on the stoop with her hands folded, and looked up when I came walking in. Even from a distance I could see worry in her eyes.

She did not rise when I reached her, so I sat down at her side. For many long moments, neither of us spoke.

Then she said, "You are registered in the church records. At least, I assume 'tis you and not some ancestor. I find it difficult to believe you could be more than two hundred years old."

"Do you?"

"Most men are glad to see eighty. Then again," she said carefully, "you are not most men, or entirely human."

"Faeries age slowly and live for centuries."

"How many centuries?"

I shrugged. "Who can tell? Anyway, I am not all faerie."

She reached into her pocket and extracted a small piece of paper. "Can you read?" she asked me.

"Aye." Maisie had taught me, during those endless days out on Dartmoor.

"Then read this," Jenny instructed. "I asked the parson to write it down for me, to be sure I got it exactly right. Stillskin, not Stills. And first name, Paul. Is that you?"

Ah, and had I been caught by the clever Jenny? Yet no one, save Mallie, would know the part of my name Sir had bestowed.

"The reason I think this must be you," she went on when I didn't speak, "is the record was given by a Mistress Martha Stillskin—for a found child. She is the woman who raised you, no?"

"She raised me, aye."

"So this—" Jenny flicked the paper "—is you."

"Will you give Maisie that name?"

"How can I do otherwise? I feel a certain measure of loyalty to you, aye. That of—of friendship. But I feel far more for her, having known her most my life. Besides, this thing you do is wrong. It is despicable that you would threaten to take her child from her."

"'Tis despicable that she lied to me."

"Have you never lied to anyone, when you were desperate?"

I had, hundreds of times. I'd lied to Sir in order to escape a swatting and to Ma in an effort to duck chores. But the bond between me and Mallie—me and

Maisie—demanded more than lies.

Bleakly, I said, "I knew her before, you see. Two centuries ago. She was taken from me cruelly, and far too soon. Before she died, she made me a promise that she'd return." I swallowed the lump in my throat. "Now she has returned, but she does not remember me or the promise. I will do whatever I must to make her recall."

"How do you know that Maisie is your lover returned?"

"I need only look at her to see it. She must see me, in return."

"Ah, but you go about it the wrong way, Master Stillskin. You will only succeed in making her hate you."

Mallie could never hate me. But then again, Mallie would never have lied to me.

Jenny did a surprising thing, reaching out and touching my hand. Her fingers clasped mine loosely, yet—as when she'd kissed me—warmth spread from the place of contact.

"Love is hard," she whispered. "So is remembering. You can force neither. Do not continue with this disastrous course, so I beg."

"Will you give her the name from the church records?" I asked again.

And once more she replied, "I must."

"Tell her I will come to her this night, for the first of her three guesses." I rose from the stoop, and Jenny came up with me. "And, Mistress Jenny—that name you have written on your slip of paper, that is not my whole name."

She drew her fingers from mine and grief flooded her eyes. "No matter—we still have two more chances.

I may yet find out the rest of it."

"Only one person on earth, besides me, knows that name."

****

As before, I sent a sleeping spell in ahead of me before appearing in Queen Maisie's bedchamber that night. I had no doubt there would be guards outside. And, even if she had not told Alfred all the truth, she might well have invited him to the room with her as a kind of defense.

But when I arrived, I saw that Maisie occupied the chamber alone. This time, since she expected me, she remained fully clothed in a gown of soft green. And this time no ruffled basket stood at hand. She'd lodged the babe elsewhere.

When I transported in, she stood already on her feet, hands clasped and fully prepared. Her eyes turned at once flinty and cold.

"Where is your child?" I asked, my gaze scanning the room.

"Nowhere you can find her."

"She is somewhere in the castle?"

"Perhaps."

"You think you can protect her by hiding her from me. Yet my thoughts—like my person—can go anywhere."

"I care not. I don't want you so much as looking at her."

Doubt twisted my heart then, I will admit it. But putting a hard edge on my voice, I said, "Twice have you made promises to me and failed to keep them. You must now fulfill the obligation."

"By remembering your name."

"Aye."

"How many guesses am I permitted this night, Master Peddler?"

"Three."

A cunning look—one such as Mallie had never in her life worn—invaded Maisie's eyes. She had sent Jenny out searching on her behalf, aye. But did she know Jenny then came to speak with me? That she confided in me or that we had what might be considered a friendship?

Had Jenny told her she'd discovered but part of my name?

I could not tell. But I could almost feel Jenny whispering now in my ear. *Show her mercy.*

My heart, though, contained little mercy at that moment. I was, after all, half faerie, and such are not known for their kindness.

So I said, "You will have three chances to speak my name, mistress, on each of the next three nights, when I come to you. Three, to save your child."

She drew herself up. She wound her fingers together and the cunning expression in her lovely eyes deepened. "Is it…Robin Longbottom?" she guessed.

"It is not."

"Ah. Unfortunate." She held up a finger. "Is it Julian Underhill?"

"Nay."

Another finger went into the air. Her gaze grew sharp enough to cut tinder. "Ah, then I perceive it must be Paul Stillskin."

So Jenny had not told her all. For a fleeting instant, I wondered why. But my anger—and let it be admitted, disappointment—was far too great to allow for other emotions.

For an instant, I let Maisie think she had won. I pulled a long face and incipient victory shone in her eyes.

"That is three," I said softly.

"And I'm right with the last one, aye? I have guessed! You will go away, and leave me and my daughter alone."

For the space of several heartbeats, I let her enjoy her supposed victory. Then, with mock sorrow, I shook my head. "But that is not the whole of my name."

She looked so crestfallen I almost regretted it. Why, I asked myself again, had Jenny not warned her? Had the little brown hen hoped that, at the last, mercy might enter my heart?

Such was hope, a commodity upon which I'd been living far too long.

I said slowly and clearly, repeating it, "That is not my whole name."

Consternation seized her. As before, she went pale and rosy by turns. "Ah!" she cried. "What, then? What more is there to it?"

"That, you must remember."

"I cannot." She balled her hands into fists. "Do you not suppose I have tried?"

"Try harder, unless you wish for me to take your child."

Wish, wish.

"Never. I will do whatever I must to protect her. Lie, cheat—I will kill you first."

Those terrible words rang in my ears and made me shudder. For the first time, I wanted to be away from her.

Mallie, my sweet Mallie.

I followed the impulse and left the place, transporting out with speed back to the downs, where I walked for the balance of the night.

I vowed she would not get the better of me, no matter what else might happen.

Chapter Twenty-Five

Strangely, amid all the distress of it and the tangle of emotions that filled me, Jenny's words kept returning to my mind over and over again. She'd warned me that if I held to my intentions, Maisie would come to hate me. I did not want to warrant it, despite what I'd now seen in the queen's eyes.

I half expected Jenny to be waiting for me again when I came walking home at daybreak, possibly because she'd been so much on my mind. When no small brown figure met my gaze, I imagined her scrambling for more information about me, perhaps seeking to comfort her distraught mistress, bidding her to remember.

Remember, I whispered into the clear air that flowed over the downs from the sea. *Know me.*

I did not see Mistress Jenny all that endless day. I wracked my brains trying to think was there any written record of the name Sir, drunk on his favorite beverage, had given me? Certainly, no one left alive would remember it.

Only Mallie.

The weather turned filthy before nightfall. Wind and storm blew in from the ocean; when I popped into the queen's chamber, I could hear the rain beating against the stone walls and the shuttered window.

This time Maisie appeared neither composed nor

confident. Her golden-brown hair, spilling wild and unconfined down her back, looked as if she'd been busy dragging her fingers through it. Her expression, when she saw me, turned distracted.

Once more the child had been excluded from the meeting. No matter. I'd located her with my thoughts. She, like most everyone else in the castle, lay beneath a spell of sleep.

"Good evening," I greeted Maisie, and gave a bow that seemed to horrify rather than charm her. "And have you, madam, come to see the error of your ways?"

She clutched her skirts in both hands and took a step backward, away from me. Her eyes burned like two blue coals in her face. "What error?"

"You should never have made a promise you did not mean to keep, and you never should have lied to me. The old man who raised me said liars cannot prosper."

"I am sorry, then. Truly I am. Surely you can see I was desperate and would have done anything, said anything. But that is all you shall have of me. Go away, vile creature! Just go and leave me be."

Vile creature? Others had called me that, but Mallie, never. She'd been able to see past the shell that enfolded me to the heart within.

Anger hardened my heart against her once again. I'd almost been willing to offer her a measure of mercy. Almost. But if she could not remember, I could not forget.

I drew myself up. "We have an agreement, and you shall hold to it. Tell to me my name."

"Roger. It is Roger Paul Stillskin."

A cold smile stretched my lips. "It is not."

Fear stirred in her eyes. "It is Master Markam Paul Stillskin. You are named after the old man you mention, the one who raised you."

Had that been Sir's given name? Fancy I had not known it. I shook my head. "That is no more my complete name than what you offered me last time."

"Paul Stillskin Smuggler, then. That's what you do for a living."

Ah, and Jenny had been busy. For I could not imagine the queen running about the kingdom discovering such information on her own.

Sternly, I told her, "You are meant to remember my name, not present me with those others give you."

"I cannot! Don't you see that, you stupid creature? I can't remember you. I never knew you, and I do not wish to know you now."

Before I could speak, she hurried on, "I have a life here, a good life. Better than anything of which I could dream. I have a sweet little lass, like a rosebud she is, and you are ruining it all. Oh, why can't you just go and leave us be?"

"Because I want back what we had together."

"We had nothing. Do you not suppose I'd remember an association with such a cruel, evil demon?"

That caused me to shudder within, though I revealed no sign. Instead, I accused, "I heard you. I overheard you singing one of my songs."

"What songs?"

"One of those I made for you, long ago. No one else could have that tune in her head, in her heart. If you remember that, why can't you remember me?"

She looked baffled. My stubborn, battered heart

wavered, prey to sudden doubt. So long ago—what if she never did remember? What would be left in my life save a hard road of endless days, stretching to a future I could not contemplate?

Insupportable, to live long, linger on and on, never having my one desire.

She cried, "I remember no songs. That is, Jenny and I used to sing tunes all day long on the farm, to make the chores go easier. Everyone knows those old tunes."

"No one else knows this one."

"I despair, Master Stillskin. I will never be able to give you what you request. Have you no kindness in your heart?"

"You have one more chance," I told her, unflinching. "One more visit tomorrow night."

She lifted her chin. "If you take our daughter, I will tell my husband all."

"He will disown you."

"Maybe. Maybe not. Either way, he will come after you with all his men. They will hunt you all across the downs like a rabid fox, and he will get our daughter back."

"Not if I hide her by magic."

"I have heard when a faerie dies, his spell breaks. We will find her after you are killed."

Now I recoiled. What had I done that Mallie—my sweet darling girl—should speak of wanting me dead? Aye, Jenny had warned me. But I hadn't believed it possible.

Over our heads, thunder rumbled loud enough to bring the stones of the castle down.

I hissed at Maisie, very like the father I'd never

known, "You have one more chance, madam, only one."

****

Numb, I sat in the rain until dawn. I no longer cared much what happened to me—I'd seen the future in Maisie's eyes.

With daylight, the rain slackened. I went inside and built a fire in the hearth. I felt weak and unwell; I didn't know what to do.

For good or ill, it would all end tonight. I wondered what I should do with the babe when I got her here. For I did not believe Maisie would come up with my name, nor that Jenny would discover it for her.

Maisie remembered me not, because she did not want to remember. That realization felt like a dagger sunk deep into my heart. She was happy with her new life, she who meant everything in the world to me.

I tended the fire all that day long, in part to keep warm, as the weather outside remained misty and chill, and in part so I could watch the pictures in the flames. The fire showed me all sorts of things that day, pictures of myself and Mallie together, laughing, teasing, being comfortable—and comforting—as only two true lovers can be. Were they pictures of my future, or of what I would never have again?

Had even my friend, the fire, turned on me?

What preparations I made for my trip to the castle that night! My last chance. The moment that would either free me or end it all. In my heart, though, I knew already which it would be, and my grief fair consumed me.

Wishes are powerful things. So are beliefs. If you learn nothing else from my story, learn that. I might wish that Maisie would, at the last possible instant, remember me. But I no longer believed it would happen.

I believed I did not deserve love—down at the root of my soul, I did. But I carefully combed my hair, which stuck out from my head like the feathers of a black bird, covering my ears, and brushed my coat, and even cleaned the mud of the downs from my boots.

So much did I want her to love me.

I went with no glamour—the real me, over two hundred years old and looking but one score and five or so. No disguises this time. No more hiding.

See me. Love me again.

Chapter Twenty-Six

Maisie met me on her feet, once more well-dressed and exquisitely groomed. If I had dropped all pretenses, she had donned hers like armor, preparing for this final confrontation.

Seeing her again, standing with her head high and her eyes glowing impossibly blue, golden-brown hair tumbling down her back, reminded me so much of Mallie it started an ache inside. Just so might Mallie have posed upon a tussock, making a bow to me or dancing to one of my tunes. For an instant, then, time blurred, one image bleeding into the other so I neither knew nor cared where I stood.

"Ah, Master Peddler," she said as soon as I appeared. "I have been awaiting you."

Her confidence gave me pause. Did she merely think to hold onto her dignity? Did she think acting the part of the queen would send me away?

I bowed to her and she curtsied to me, still retaining that dangerous gleam in her eyes.

"As you see—" She swept the room with a gesture "—my daughter is not here."

"I can feel her and know where she is."

"It does not matter. Her presence will not be needed here this night. I know your name."

"Do you?" My mind raced as it had before. Did she? Could she?

"Aye, but I believe I still get three guesses, do I not?"

"If you wish."

Wish, wish.

"Oh I do, I do, Master Peddler. After all the agony you have caused me, the worry and the sleepless nights. You have made it impossible to enjoy my daughter's arrival in the world. I will have my three guesses, in return."

"Go ahead."

"Hmm." She pressed a slim, beringed finger to her lips. "Some names do come to mind. Are you…Samuel Paul Stillskin?"

"I am not."

"Not Samuel Paul Stillskin?" she repeated.

"I am not," I told her with emphasis. Two more. Two to go.

"Oh, have I failed again? But you have three names, am I right? Three separate names, as I have suggested."

I said nothing. Fear and hope together gripped me by the throat. Had she remembered after all? But the look in her blue eyes reflected only spite.

"I think your name is…Whiskey Paul Stillskin."

My heart stood still; for an instant I could not breathe.

"Do not be cruel," I whispered, but she didn't hear me. Already she prepared for her final guess, raised up on her tiptoes and glared at me.

"No—no, I am wrong again. Your name—your true name, you horrid little man, is Rum Paul Stillskin."

She pronounced it with such glee, such raw enjoyment and anger, I could not mistake it for anything other than what it was—a curse, a means of breaking our unwanted connection. No love rested here, no remembering.

I—Rum Paul Stillskin—did not deserve her love.

"Well? Am I right?" She threw back her head and laughed in delight. "No need to answer. I can see it in your ugly face. Your torment of me is over, you terrible demon. Be gone with you! I want never to see you more."

"But, but…" I began to stammer. I leaped forward and seized her arm. She reacted as if the touch of my fingers burned her, for she recoiled and cried out.

"Do not touch me. Be gone from me, I say."

But I refused to let go. Instead I gazed straight into the hate that filled her eyes. "You must have remembered me. How else would you know my true name?"

She laughed again, cruelly. "Perhaps it is magic. You have lost, demon. Better go!"

I released her and stood swaying, having received a death blow. In her eyes, for the first time, I saw a woman I did not recognize.

Barely did I have the strength to transport out of there. Had the guards awakened and come into the chamber then, they would have taken me, helpless as a child, and the powers alone know what they would have done with me after hearing the queen's story.

But I got out, and landed where I neither knew nor cared. Dark, wind, driving pricks of rain—I barely felt them. I stumbled forward a few paces, and the rough grass and stone of the downs met my feet. Like one mortally injured, I fell to my knees.

How long I remained so, huddled down with the

rain battering me and my cheek smashed into the earth of that place, I cannot say. Pain overwhelmed me. If I could have sunk into the ground, let it swallow me up, absorb and dissolve me, I would have.

I had no reason left to live. I'd been born unwanted and would die so. Love, that precious treasure which had once been mine, was meant for others—hence I'd lost it and would be loved never more.

My own name echoed in my head. Rum Paul Stillskin, Rum Paul Stillskin. How had she learned it, if not by remembering?

She could not have remembered what we were to each other and still hate me.

I huddled where I was, collapsed onto the ground. Days and nights may have passed, for all I know. Eventually, light returned to the world and shone warm on my back. Birds sang a delicate, aching song that reverberated far over the downs.

Away, away, away...

I still breathed. I might not want to, but I did. My heart beat in my chest. As I'd been denied love, I'd been denied escape into the oblivion of death.

I got onto my feet, unsteady at first, and wandered. I kept seeing the look in Maisie's eyes—spiteful and hating. My heart hurt with every beat. Unthinking, I tramped the downs without cease, wishing the ancient land would take me back into it, from whence I had come.

A week likely passed, two weeks, a month.

When unbearable hunger seized me, I ate what I could find.

When exhausted, I fell down wherever I was and slept.

Living, like time, lost all meaning.

Mallie did not want me, would never want me. And I wanted nothing else.

Chapter Twenty-Seven

Who is so blind as one who will not see?

I came to myself with those words in my ears, and raised my head in an effort to determine my situation.

Dim light flickered in from above, and the cloying smell of damp soil and chilly stone surrounded me.

I lay in a grave.

Ah, perhaps I'd died after all, perished from a shattered heart. Perhaps I'd succeeded in crawling into the earth and losing myself in her bosom.

Then why did I fail to remain dead?

Because a bird sang a melody of pure and piercing sweetness. It filtered into the grave where I lay, penetrated my ears, and wove a spell inside my head.

One of calling.

Wish, wish, wish.

I knew the song. That, and not its sweetness alone, had roused me. My ears hauled me up, and my heart commanded me to unfold myself from the chilly ground and to gaze with newly opened eyes.

At first I saw nothing. I occupied a kistvaen, one of the pit graves that dot the downs, and could not see far in any direction. Just green moss and stone, a wild sky of deep blue, and unfettered clouds roaming.

How could a bird sing a song I knew?

Because, my brain stirred and informed me, that was no bird I heard, but a woman's voice.

I climbed up out of the earth in which I'd gone aground, stood on my feet for the first time in days, and gazed around.

The beauty of the downs fair blinded me. Place of my birth, place of my heart. But it lay uninhabited. I could see no woman who might be singing there.

Yet I could hear her still. A voice high and clear. The song, gentle and yearning, rose and fell and tapped into all the longing within me. It brought tears to my eyes.

Where is the love of my heart?
I have searched for him, searched and searched.
My love, so long from me apart.
Ne'er will I cease though the world may end.
I have wished for him, wished and wished
For my one love and friend.

Aye, I knew the tune. I'd created it not far from this very place on just such a day as this while Mallie and I lounged on our backs, fingers linked, counting the fluffy sheep that roamed the sky. The words, however, were new—and not mine.

Curiosity made me step out of the kistvaen onto the stones that edged the ancient tomb, and a breeze caught me, streaming my hair back from my face.

I espied...

A woman approaching me from the west. It must be afternoon, for the sun, full in my eyes, kept me from seeing her clearly. I saw only a gleam of brown, catching the sun's rays, and the flicker of a white apron.

I heard Mallie's voice.

I felt Mallie's presence.

For an instant I went breathless with the need to believe—with the inability to believe. Then I stretched onto my tiptoes, perched there on the stone. I raised my arms and waved.

She saw me. She stilled her voice and froze for a fraction of time before she ran to me with her arms outstretched, ran just the way Mallie used to when we'd been too long apart.

She hit me like a small gale wind, and knocked me back off the curb. My arms closed fast around her, and we both tumbled into the grave.

There we lay, with her atop me, her breath and mine both loud in my ears. My arms crushed her to me; her palms flew up to cradle my face. With careful fingers, she brushed the place where the iron had burned and scarred my skin so long ago.

"Oh, my love, what did they do to you?" For an instant, sorrow filled her eyes. "I looked for you so long, Rum Paul. I searched and searched, and had nearly given up. I believed you lost."

"You searched for me?"

"Aye, long—long."

"How long?"

"Weeks."

"Weeks?" I questioned, like one in a daze.

"It is nearly midsummer."

"Yet you did not give up." The truth of it trickled into me, slowly as the return of warmth after a hard winter. Did I dare believe?

She told me, "I would never cease looking for you, never. Did I not promise to return?"

All the breath fled my body then. No matter—I had no need of breath. I gazed into her brown-speckled eyes, brimming with magic, and stammered, "You? It was you, all this while, and never Maisie?"

"Aye, and I could not make you see it. For quite some time, I did not know it either, only that I felt drawn to you, and needed to be near you, needed to make my home in your heart. You were so set upon winning Maisie you barely noticed me. I hope—" She dropped a kiss on my lips "—you are not—" Another kiss "—disappointed?"

"That is not a word I would use to describe this moment."

"How would you describe it?"

I searched my mind and my heart before I told her honestly, "There is no word, Jenny. No word for this."

A small smile curled her lips—a woman's smile full of knowledge and mystery. Light danced in her eyes. "Well," she allowed, "mayhap one."

"What is that?" I gasped, realizing what I beheld in her now was Mallie's light, Mallie's love.

She kissed me once more, hard, before she said, "I believe this must be the very definition of irony."

****

"You kept telling Maisie to see you—to remember you," Jenny said a short time later, when we'd crawled from the kistvaen and sat together on a tussock, in the wind. We'd linked fingers, weaving them together just as we used to long ago, in days when I asked nothing more from the world than her presence. "But you never truly looked at me."

I raised her fingers to my lips and kissed them. "You arc right. I kept thinking because Maisie looked so much like Mallie, and came from the same family, she must be the one I'd waited for so long. Can you forgive me?"

She once more smiled, and it was Mallie's smile,

pure and without pretense. "Always. I will forgive you always, anything."

I should have known, I told myself then. Why hadn't I sensed the truth from the steadfastness of her spirit?

I released her hand, but only so I could cradle her face between my palms. I spoke directly to her heart. "I am sorry. Sorry I wasted so much time. Sorry I failed to know you at once. Such a fool, me!"

"Such a dear, beloved fool."

We kissed, and the warmth of it lit me, rescued me from the dark where I'd lived so long. I could have gone on so forever, breathing her breath, but my mind seemed to have followed me back to life, and I had questions.

Gently I put her from me and asked, "How did you know? How, when I failed to? Surely you did not remember me at once?"

She shook her head. "I felt drawn to you, fascinated by you as never by anyone else. I felt attracted to you and wanted nothing so much as to be out here with you on the downs, every chance I got."

"I wish you had told me."

Wish.

"Would you have listened? Would you have believed me, if you did?" She touched my face lovingly. "You did not believe, even, that you deserved love. I think that broke my heart most of all. Not only did you fail to see me, you failed to see what I saw when I looked at you."

"What is that?"

"The magic that runs through this place I love so dearly. You are like the downs, walking—your eyes are like the moss that hides in the clefts of the rocks. Your hair is like the sky at night, and there's a wildness in you that I crave. You are fragile and strong, and my love for you is as endless and enduring as this place." Tears flooded her eyes. "You waited two centuries for me."

"And," I vowed, "would have waited till the end of all time."

Chapter Twenty-Eight

"Tell me the truth," I whispered in Jenny's ear. Night had fallen. We lay side by side, flat on our backs while looking up at the stars, our fingers again entwined. "You still have not said how you came to know who I was, and who you were to me."

"It did not come all at once, that knowing. A woman does not dream her true love has been waiting more than two hundred years for her to keep a promise—especially a simple woman like me. But it seems I came into this world yearning for something, and when I saw you the longing eased for the very first time.

"Not until Maisie sent me round about, seeking after your name, did the pieces begin to fall together for me. All throughout the district there are stories of you—at least of someone who might be you, if I could believe a man might live so long. Yet it became clear you were something more than just a man."

"Maisie called me a demon."

"Maisie does not know you as I do. She does not love you as I do."

That made me turn my head and look at her. "You are the only one who has ever been able to see past my appearance. How did you come to realize what we once were to each other?"

"I think it was the song."

"Eh?" That startled me.

"Maisie told me you accused her of being the one you sought because you heard her singing a song, one you had made."

"For Mallie."

"For me. What she didn't tell you, for she likely did not remember, is she learned that tune from me. We used to sing it while going about our chores on the farm. But it belonged, always, to me. The same way I came into the world wanting you, I think I came into the world carrying your music."

I lay silent, cradling her fingers, staring in wonder at the stars. "So then you—remembered me?"

"'Tis more as if I recalled that I'd never forgotten you. Of course, by then you had laid your intentions at Maisie's feet. I wanted to tell you, but I feared you wouldn't believe me. I also feared you wanted her instead of me, and would be…well, disappointed. She is so beautiful. Every man who's ever seen her has wanted her."

"You are beautiful beyond measure, beyond description."

She rolled onto her side so she could face me. "It was I who recalled your name. It came to me on that last day, when she was so desperate and she sent me to search the church records again. It resounded so clear in my head, Rum Paul Stillskin. It was I who told Maisie, and so confounded you. I hope you can forgive me."

I faced her also. "I forgive you, forever and always." I echoed her words. "I never wanted the child, by any road. I merely wanted a hold on her that would bring her to me."

"And now, my fine Rum Paul?"

"I want a hold on you."

"You have one. And what of the future?"

"I wish the queen happiness of her husband and child."

"And what of us? Is there nothing you would ask me?"

"Stay with me."

"Here? Tonight?"

"Here—tonight, tomorrow, always. Live here with me, wild as the hares and the grouse."

Light danced in her speckled, brown eyes. "Wild as the wind," she whispered, her lips nearly touching mine.

Wish.

"I have the farm. I have a good occupation running the still. I can keep us."

"Two misfits, together?"

"Two halves, making one perfect whole."

Believe.

"It sounds well to me." And she presented her lips to me, in a vow. "Shall there be magic?" she asked when the kiss ended.

"Magic will bind us one to the other."

"Shall there be songs?"

"Songs shall gladden us."

"And"—her voice broke—"shall there be love?"

"That," I promised, "most of all."

The years have passed swiftly. We have lived many seasons on our farm, have worked hard to improve it—aye, even I who once shirked every chore so assiduously. The hardest work, so I've learned, goes easier in Jenny's company.

We have three children, two lads and a lass, all

with a measure of faerie blood in their veins, all capable of deep love.

Only while holding them in my arms did I realize in full how cruelly I'd tormented Maisie. Despite her past friendship with Jenny, I have not seen the queen since that last awful meeting in her bedchamber, when she spoke my true name. I have kept her secret—her husband, the king, still thinks her the miraculous lass who spun straw into gold for him—and she has kept mine.

The world ages slowly, I a bit less so, my beloved Jenny less slowly still. Every night when we go to our bed and lie there side by side, she links her fingers through mine and says, "I know I will not live as long as you will, my love. Promise you will wait for me."

And I return, "You know I will."

"I promise to return to you again and again, and again—no matter how long it may take."

And I know, deep in my heart, I will wait for her as long as it takes, just as the downs await the new sun each dawning. For I, Rum Paul Stillskin, still deserve her love.

A word about the author…

Multi award-winning author Laura Strickland delights in time traveling to the past and searching out settings for her books, be they historical romance, steampunk, or something in between.

Born and raised in western New York, she's pursued lifelong interests in lore, legend, magic, and music, all reflected in her writing. Although she enjoys travel, she's usually happiest at home, not far from Lake Ontario, with her husband.

Author of numerous historical and contemporary romances, she is the creator of the Buffalo Steampunk Adventure series set in her native city.

Thank you for purchasing
this publication of The Wild Rose Press, Inc.

For questions or more information
contact us at
info@thewildrosepress.com.

The Wild Rose Press, Inc.
www.thewildrosepress.com

To visit with authors of
The Wild Rose Press, Inc.
join our yahoo loop at
http://groups.yahoo.com/group/thewildrosepress/